Almost BRILLIANT

TK Cassidy

ACKNOWLEDGEMENTS

This book is the result of my first NaNoWriMo (National Novel Writing Month) competition held internationally in November every year. As daunting a task as writing 50,000 words in 30 days but the job is also rewarding. Thanks to the support of all the great people I met and wrote with. Word wars, virtual and real write-ins, supportive emails, someone who knows what you mean to talk to at 3 AM. Priceless!! I will do this again and again.

Special thanks to Angie Smith, Dr. E. Thomas Lewis and Dr. James Zuppa and their staffs for helping me think out ideas and to Diana Sharples for continually staying just out of reach as we raced to finish our novels in time! The challenge made the job just that much more enjoyable!

And very special thanks to my friend and colleague Rayda Reed, without whom I wouldn't even know about NaNoWriMo... yes, Rayda, we are still friends!

Thanks also to Lisa "Sunshine" Musil for an excellent "last going over". And another round of thanks to Becky Shiner Stong, my SIL, for her fresh eyes and good comments in the last go 'round. And my long-time supporter, Jennifer Rush

And as always, my abiding love for MSB (Dale Fleming). You are the best part of my life!

product of the author's imagination or are used fictionally. Any resemblance to actual persons, living or dead, events or locales is entirely coincidental.

Cover illustration by Diana L. Sharples

For more information, visit the author's Amazon page: TK Cassidy Amazon Author Page

For even more information,

Visit the author's website: TKCassidyWrites.com

CHAPTER

Now let me try to explain here. My odd little story is a strange, and I think an even unique, one. I'm sure you have heard other writers say the same thing, but I promise that this tale will make you scratch your head more than once. At first glance, you might think this is just another story of never-ending greed and grisly plans of murder. But neither was my intention ... that's not who I am. I know, every criminal in every jail says that. They didn't commit the crime. The whole miserable escapade was a misunderstanding, an accident or someone else setting them up. And, when you hear my totally true story, you'll think I am just another lazy useless old fool trying to cruise through the end of my life; trying to get something for nothing. Well, that's kind of true... but that's not the whole story!

When you find yourself alone and homeless at the ripe old age of 90 and then someone offers you more than you ever thought you would have, you simply do what you gotta do! I mean, I was just taking care of myself, or trying to, doing a pretty good job of it and ... well, that's when everything went eyelashes over toe jam!

Maybe, I should start by telling you how I ended up where I am and with this leg in a cast. By the way, I'm expecting a guest in a few minutes. He already knows all about me but let me fill you in while we school with the guy who's coming over. In fact, I went to school with all the people I'll be telling you about soon.

I forgot to tell you another important detail, by the way. I'm in the local jailhouse. The reason will soon be very apparent. I should be in another house if fate had been on my side and, when you hear about how everything conspired against me, you'll understand and maybe even be on my side. I have been told that a clear conscience is usually the sign of a bad memory. My memory is just fine! And my conscience is clear as the proverbial bell. Everyone else is struggling with what happened because they don't know what actually happened. That's why my story needs to be told. That's why the reporter is coming to see me today.

My soon-to-arrive visitor is a big mucky muck in this town. He went to some fancy school back East and got himself a fine journalism degree. He even wrote for a couple big newspapers before he came back to this dinky little place. Everybody treats him like a shining star because he writes a guest column in the local paper now and then

... when he feels like writing. I bet he'll feel like taking this project on when he hears the whole story. After all, he gave me my nickname back in grade school.

Oh my, I do believe I forgot my manners. My name is Durwood P. Loudon. Everyone calls me Scabby. I know, Scabby is not the best name with which to be saddled, but I like that one a lot more than Durwood. I was given the nickname Scabby for two reasons actually. When I was little, my feet seemed to find every freshly dug hole, rotting stick, loose rock, lump of mud, and errant dust bunny to trip over. I never walked when I could run full-out and I never ran when I could jump from launch pad to landing space. I continually had skinned up knees and elbows for the first seven years of my life! I used to pick at those scabs until they bled and healed over and everyone noticed. That's how I got my nickname. Believe me, that name was better than Durty or Woody or anything else with which they tried to stick me! Later, the nickname took on a much different meaning, but the title still fit me fine. I just never tried to outgrow the nickname.

Being an orphan and all, there weren't too many people interested in making me do the things I should do. As long as I was home after school, did my chores and was in bed for bed check, I was pretty much on my own with the other kids that lived in the state home. I was traded out to foster homes a couple times but I usually made my way back to the cold brick building I called home within a month or two. Like I said, I wasn't a mean kid or a bad kid. I just had trouble fitting what I thought was right into what everyone else thought was right.

A lot of my friends and classmates went on to do big things like this fancy-pants reporter that is coming. I told you he was a reporter, right? Oh well, I will now. I think I'll just call him Mr. Fancy Britches Reporter from now on. I never tried to leave this little burg. I liked this small hometown feel of a place where everyone knew everyone else and nothing really changed much. I just never felt the urge to leave like so many others. Never was what you might call eat up with ambition. I just wanted to get through life the best I could. This town fits my style just right.

What I didn't like was school. Having to get all dressed up every day – just so. Having to sit in little oaken desks in straight lines – just so. Having to walk in a straight line with your hands behind your back and a bubble in your mouth everywhere – just so. Having to speak correctly – just so... Write properly – just so. Breathe quietly through your nose – just so. All those "just so's" really rubbed me the wrong way. To my feeble way of thinking, a person had to have a danged poor mind if they can't think of more than one way to spell any old word or do anything for that matter! The world is all about being different, they said. Be yourself, they said. But be the same as everyone else, too.

The teachers were always telling kids when to talk, when to need the restroom. And then after all those "have to's", they turn around and test you on all the other things they said! I mean really, if you are going to go be a doctor or a lawyer or something, you need all that. But I knew when I was young that I was staying right here, and I'd never need much of that stuff.

The only thing I liked about school was reading. I found out about those black marks on the page in first grade, how they fit with the pictures and then how, if you squished them together, they meant words and you could read them. After that, no one could keep me away from books. I read everything in every classroom I was ever in and all the books, both fiction and nonfiction, in the library. Then I discovered a little bit of heaven on earth called the public library. If I wanted to go to that library, I had to walk more than two miles each way, but to be able to sit in a corner and be left alone to read was pure heaven to me. I always had a bookmarked book or two in my pockets.

When I got older, folks used to make snide comments about my way of speaking. Now, I know a lot of big words. People would make remarks about me trying to make myself seem bigger than I was, but I got the words from well-written books, looking up new words in the big old moldy-smelling dictionary on the podium in the library, and using them when I got the chance. If people thought I was being snooty, well, that was their problem.

School and I parted ways as soon as I was big enough to lie about my age and get jobs. I was about 13. After that, I could always get jobs and I worked as often as I could. I was good at hauling things, shoveling things, moving things and lifting things. I could paint a house in a day or drive a tractor over fields until the earth was turned and the seed was sown as well as any man. Mostly, I was good at following orders.

Bosses liked me because they would tell me to do something and they knew they could count on the job being done the right way – their way. The fact of the matter was, if you wanted to pay me, I'd do the work. I may not have seen the need for schooling, but I learned early you need money for important things. Important things change as you age, but somehow enough money always gets to your pockets if you are willing to work. Sometimes a little extra ... but always enough.

About those important things I just mentioned. When I got to be about 15, I realized the most important things I wanted to be a part of always seemed to happen on Friday or Saturday nights ... if you get my drift. I learned to drink while hanging out with the other day laborers, all of them older than me. At first, they thought getting the kid drunk was funny but, when I got older, I was another source of cash to chip in and add to the all-night party. Then I was expected to pay my own way. I learned little about drugs too, but that was never my thing. Mostly I figured out that if you wanted to party all weekend, you better work hard all week. The guys didn't like you hanging around when you couldn't, hmm, shall we say, contribute to the fun.

The most important thing I learned was the truth about women. They like money. They like nice things. They like men and they like nice men, but they will even hang out with not-so-nice guys if the man has enough money.

Oh, and I did learn to like the ladies. My first crush was in first grade. Marcia Marie Hemming liked me as well as I liked her. We were kind of an item all through grade school, off and on. I reckon, if I had liked her more than beer and partying, I would have had a very different life. But she never could make me see the good side of the "just so" way to live. I'll never forget.... oh, sorry, that's a story for a later time when Mr. Fancy Britches Reporter gets here.

Where was I? Oh right. There were several

ladies that taught me things, like how a girl likes you much better after a shower and a shave. If you just want to hang out with the boys all night, you can go to the bar right out of the fields or off the site. The guys don't even care if you brush your teeth, comb your hair or even change your clothes but, if you want a lady to spend time with you, there are rules to be followed. Again, with the rules. Life has so daggone many rules.

Hold up! Did you hear that? Yup, I think my guest is being shown to my room. This is gonna be good. I can't wait to see ole Mr. Fancy Britches Reporter's face when he hears my tale. I bet he never thought in his wildest dreams that he would be writing about me like he did all those really important stories for that big city newspaper. No, sirree Bob. Well here and now, I am the big story. I haven't been getting many visitors and my trial won't be here for a few weeks so I am going to make the telling of this story last a long time.

I've been a prisoner here for a couple days.

Not sure how long I'll stay; might be the rest of my life. That would be OK. Did you ever see an old television show called *Mayberry RFD*? That is sort of how this small-town jail looks. In order to get a clear picture of my lovely abode, you have to imagine a long, narrow room made of concrete blocks on three sides with an iron cot with a thin mattress for a bed and bars along the open side. No seating for guests, but then, like I said, I've never had any that wanted to come in and sit. In the corner behind a low brick wall is the toilet and a wash basin. Of course, they don't let me use the can in here for important business. The men's room is just down the hall. The sheriff is always glad to let me go down there after his first experience with my, uhm, shall we say contribution to the compost pile.

Pete's the sheriff. He's an OK guy. I can tell that he doesn't really believe all the things they are saying about me and that helps my case. I went to school with his dad, Marty. In fact, Marty and I had some history going back to elementary school and the time I stood up for him in a certain restroom by the gym. Several big guys decided it would be funny to take Marty into that bathroom and give him a "swimming" lesson. I saw what was happening and raced in to help him get out of that situation. Scoff if you want. I may be little, but I have always been tough. Besides, I usually had surprise on my side! We have been friends since that day. I hated the day Marty died. He was a great sheriff who often turned a bit of a blind eye when I got carried away with my favorite past times, like drinking too much, staying out too late ... but Pete was right there to take over the family legacy. Nothing changed much.

There are a couple of part-time deputies on the force that are OK guys as well. Real low key. The best thing about a small town is everyone pretty much knows who you are and, whether you mean harm or not. When they know you don't have much truck with the rules but don't try to bend them too far, there is a decided lack of enforcement over those dreaded "just so's". And I already told you how I feel about those. While I am here, as long as I stay out of the way, I can pretty much come and go as I like – inside the building, of course.

Wait a minute! The voices I heard in the office are coming down the hall. But I don't recognize one of them. Sounds like a young boy, kinda high and squeaky. I sneak a peek at the person following Pete, but he's not the reporter I was expecting. I had planned to be sitting on the cot all cool, my broken leg propped up, all suave-like and acting like I was doing Mr. Fancy Britches Reporter a favor by letting him talk to me. But, seeing the kid in Pete's wake, I struggled to my feet and yelled, "Who the devil are you bringing down here?"

Pete laughed and yelled back, "I'm bringing you your fancy reporter, Scabby, just like you asked."

He was laughing at me with the same snicker I give when I'm about to get the better of someone. I had told him about how the paper was going to send their best reporter over and do a fine big story on me. I have to admit, I was bragging a little. Told everyone who would listen how I would be remembered in the history of this town like no one ever thought I would be. I would be one important person when this story hit the stands.

But this visitor was just some kid! He looked barely old enough to be allowed in here. Watching him come down the hall was like looking at a cartoon character from the early days of cartooning. His scrawny neck seemed to strain to hold his big, wobbly head up. His bushy brown hair stuck out on its own in all directions. His legs and arms were long and boney. His hands looked like someone had stuffed their father's work gloves full of washcloths and taped them on skinny sticks. His feet looked like oval concrete blocks moving heavily as he came shuffling down the hall. I swear he tripped twice as he meandered down the linoleum floor that Danny, the janitor, kept spotlessly clean.

When they got to my door, Pete stood there with his arms over his chest. The twinkle in his eye told me that he was enjoying this situation way too much. I turned my fury on the kid. "What are you doing here? Who are you," I asked him.

He reached up a bit unsteadily, pushed his black-framed owl glasses up his nose with his middle finger and gave a nervous cough. Then he rubbed his massive hand on his scrawny thigh like he was trying to clean the sweat off. He stretched his huge hand out and said his name was Frankie, Frankie Melton. He further explained that he was the editor of the high school newspaper, but he was also a reporter in training for the town paper. He was here to write my story.

High school paper! Reporter in training!!! Daggone it!!! Thirty years ago, I'd have reached through the bars and punched him out. And then I'd have punched Pete, too, for standing there laughing like a hyena in heat too. I grabbed the bars until my knuckles turned white. "How old are you?" I growled at the pimply face kid expecting him to back up, but he held his ground and softly said, "Seventeen."

"Seventeen! Oh, for crying in a bucket! They sent me a baby! Shut up," I yelled at Pete who wasn't even bothering to try to hold his chuckling! I pushed off the bars and hobbled back to my cot. Pete opened the door, which was never locked, and let the kid in.

I growled, "Well, come on in here then." I flopped down on the iron cot with its skimpy mattress and waved him in. He was slow to step inside, one cautious step and then another, kinda like a skittish colt afraid of being trapped. I waved him in again.

"Come on in. No one is going to hurt you and Pete will let you leave whenever you want to." I pointed out that he had two choices of seating: the other end of the bed or the floor. I was going to mention the "seat" in the corner, but he didn't seem to have a sense of humor about the whole thing. Pete said he would get him a chair. I could hear the sheriff laughing all the way down the hall. I threw my meanest 'knock it off' look at his back. But, even if he had seen the look, that wouldn't have fazed Pete. It's hard to intimidate someone when you are a foot shorter, fifty pounds lighter, twice their age, and they are wearing a star and a gun.

CHAPTER

2

I leaned back against the flat pillows I had propped up against the wall. I lowered my eyes and watched the awkward kid nervously try to find an acceptable place to settle down. I knew Pete might take a while to bring him a chair so I decided to enjoy his entertaining discomfort while I could. While he still had his back to me, in my gruffest, loudest mean voice, I bellowed, "I can't believe they sent me a kid still wet behind the knees. Where's the real reporter?"

I hid my delight a little when he jumped and

dumped his satchel – honest to God, he was carrying a leather satchel – out onto the floor. He dropped to his bony knees, scrambling around to pick stuff up and stammering the whole time. All I heard was a whimpering murmur. Time to make him jump again. This might be fun after all! I yelled, "Did you hear me, Kid? Where is the real reporter?"

He looked up at me and held my hooded gaze like a frightened deer with a loaded dump truck racing straight at him. If he'd had been a cat, he'd have been hanging off the ceiling tiles with all his claws dug in. Pete would have had to pry his claws out to get him down.

Pete showed up with the rickety chair they kept in the back, pushed the seat inside and told me to behave myself. I grinned and winked at Pete but turned a hard-eyed glare at the shivery kid. Pete told him I was harmless and turned to walk away. The kid shuffled after Pete and stage-whispered that he had heard I killed a lot of people. Pete looked over his shoulder at me. I could tell he was in on the game. He turned back to the kid and whispered equally loud that I had, but not here in the jail.

I was roaring with laughter inside while watching this fidgety kid try to calm down and get set up. He kept apologizing for everything. Apparently, they wouldn't let him bring in his laptop so he had to write everything long hand. Then the tip broke off his pencil. The ancient chair was wobbly. He tried putting the legal pad on the bed and bending over to write, but that didn't seem to work for him. He even sat on the floor and tried to write on the seat of the chair but that only lasted a few seconds. Nothing seemed to be going his way. He finally pulled the chair over to the low wall and put his pad on the concrete blocks. He shook himself all around like I have seen dogs do before they settle in and seemed ready to write. From somewhere in all that hair, he pulled a pencil out from behind his ear and poised the tip over the paper. A few seconds later, he looked to his right and saw the stainless-steel toilet. I promise I never saw anyone actually turn as green as a ripe kiwi before. I guess they don't have open air toilets where he lives.

I let him stammer and stutter for a while longer. Apparently, Mr. Fancy Britches Reporter was ill and not doing well. For a brief second, my heart skipped a beat. I wondered what kind of sickness might be plaguing him. Then I remembered the other reporter was a year behind me in school. Even if he died, his death wouldn't help me. That may not make much sense to you now ... but everything will be clear soon.

"Alright," I told him, "you are boring me. Let's get this thing going. What do you want to know?"

He looked at his notes and read off all the details: my name – check; my age (did I tell you I'll be 91 next month?) – check; where I went to school – check; how I'd always lived here – check; no college – check; no career – check. I bellowed at him! "You are here to make me famous and, so far, that's all you have? Get on with it, Kid! What do you want to know?"

I was kind of impressed. This time he held his ground and didn't flinch. His answer took the wind out of my sails a bit. He said he wanted to know how a quiet shy little kid that everyone seemed to like becomes someone who tries to kill people he grew up in a place where there was nothing worth killing over. I stared at him. This time in disbelief, not intimidation, and he held my gaze.

"You're so young," I said shaking my head. "Do your notes tell you where I have been living for the past few years?"

He shuffled through the pages and shook his head.

"Try the corner of Elm and Main Street behind Olsen's City bakery ... second big box from the big black dumpster." I saw surprise in his eyes.

"You mean back where all those boxes are," he gasped. "I always thought they were just boxes being stored back there."

"You got the crust, Pie Face. I'm homeless. When you are young and healthy, you can make as much money as you want whenever you want. But then nature pulls an ugly trick on you and you get old. No one wants to hire you even though you know you can still do the jobs and suddenly making money is not so easy. You see, Kid, the worse part about getting old is once you pass get older than about 60 nobody gives two eggs out of the same hen about what you do.

"I know I'm in better shape than most people my age and a lot of the younger ones, probably because I worked so hard all my life. The one thing I have learned about life is that everything goes on despite what you do. When you get older and no longer have a way to make money, there are things worth killing for. But believe me," I said, "Maggie and I talked the idea out for a long time before we decided to do anything."

I saw sorrow in his eyes. I sat straight up,

well, as much as my leg would let me. "Like I said, I'm still pretty spry although time has taken its toll. I shook my finger at him and said don't you go getting misty on me. I don't need your sympathy. I lived my life like I wanted too; like Old Blue Eyes said, I did it my way." I looked at him hard. I swear if he had asked who Old Blues Eyes was, I'd have throttled him.

To his credit, he jotted down a note and asked who Maggie was. That made me think a bit. I missed Maggie a lot. No one had been able to find her since they pulled me in here. He waited patiently.

"I'll tell you about Maggie," I said conspiratorially. "You got nothing but time, right?" He nodded. I gestured around." Well, settle in, Kid, because that is all I have ... time."

One of my foster parents once described a long-winded person as someone who went around his ass to scratch his nose. Well, I thought as I settled into my spot again, we are going to go

around several asses before this story is finished.
I was going to have plenty of company for weeks!

CHAPTER

After he finally got his things settled and folded all those angles of arms and legs into a usable form, he looked at me as if studying a new kind of bug that had entered his space. He quietly asked how I had broken my leg.

Well, that was indeed the story, wasn't it? I told him getting my story was going to be harder than just asking. There was no way in the world anyone could understand what I had done and why – I mean, the real intricacies of the idea – in a couple of quickly told lines. No, I wanted this young man to work for my story. If they were going to send me some young pup, I was going to school him properly in the ways of the interview. I watched his fingers fidget as he watched me staring at him. I knew I didn't have him hooked yet. I needed to tell him just enough to get him really interested, but not too much so I could keep him coming back.

I dropped my gaze for a second and then looked at him out of the corner of my eye, real mysterious like, and I half whispered, "Mostly the idea came from Maggie. I never told anyone else about this part." He leaned in closer and I nodded as his eyes lit up.

"She is a good listener and comes up with great ideas." He made a note and glanced back at me, one bushy eyebrow hovering higher above his eye than the other. I gave him a knowing smile and whispered, "Maggie is the bitch I lived with."

He cocked that eyebrow even higher but didn't

shift his stare. I paused for a few seconds to keep being mysterious and then slowly continued ... "we lived together in my box behind the bakery."

Once again, he didn't flinch or ask any questions. He just laid his stubby pencil down and looked at me. I hadn't intended to tell him about Maggie yet, but now that I had opened the door, I took a long trip down memory lane. I told him just who Maggie was and how we'd met.

"Late one cold wet fall evening," I told him, "I was curled up in the back of an old washing machine box that I had found a few weeks earlier. The cardboard was thick and had some kind of plastic coating, so I was warmer and dryer than most of my fellow alley-dwellers. I had been lucky enough to score an old pallet to put under the box that same week. Keeping the box up out of the rain was an important detail I learned quickly after moving in here. Dragging the two heavy, clumsy items here had taken a lot of time, but the end result was worth the work. I guess

I could have stayed where I found the box and the pallet, but I'd found them behind a furniture shop. My chosen spot in the alley was behind a bakery. Think about it for a minute. Can you think of a warmer place than outside a bakery? When they fire up those ovens in the wee hours of the night... just about the time you think you can't stand being that cold any more ... and that glorious heat starts coming out of the vents right above you. I promise you will feel for a few minutes like you might have gone to Heaven. And one other thing, they threw away a lot of old baked goods. Breads. Donuts. Sandwiches. Stuff the bakers didn't think was fresh enough to sell. Sometimes they threw away perfectly good things just because they weren't too purty. Can you believe that? Guaranteed breakfast every day! I wasn't too keen on getting food from the dumpster at first, but hunger makes you come down off your high horse really quick.

"Like every drizzly night, I was just trying to

stay out of the rain as much as possible. But on a night like this, I couldn't control the direction of the rain ... try as I might. I had to turn the box away from the wind before I crawled in. That meant I wouldn't get the full effect of the warm oven in the morning but I had to make a choice. Dry now or warm later. Dry now won the argument every time. When I got relatively comfortable, I pulled the soggy flaps of the box down and tucked my thin, dingy blanket up closer to my chin. By blanket, I mean the old flour sacks I had poached one morning when the baker left the door open further than usual when he stepped out for his smoke break. The scratchy sacks were covered with spots and discolored places. I really tried not to ponder what the spots on the sacks might be. I just kept the cleanest parts closest to my chin ... if you get my drift. I left the bottom flap down so there would be plenty of fresh air in the box. One thing I do like is fresh air. Besides, I liked being able to smell the baked goods and know when the ovens had been turned on.

"I had just gotten settled, laying on my back, with the meager covers tugged up when I sensed something small and light slither into the furthest corner of the box. And I do mean slither. The cardboard walls of the box gave several little shudders and I thought I felt something shivering near my leg. I wasn't sure I had really felt something for a few long quiet minutes. I lay as still as a hardened sheet of ice and held my breath so long that I think my lungs cramped. During that quiet time, waiting for something to happen, my vivid imagination ran amok. I began to imagine what that might have been at my feet ... if I had really felt anything crawl in. Just when I decided that I had imagined the movement, I felt the box shudder slightly again as something bumped against the side and I heard a shaky sigh in the dark corner.

"I, of course, knew snakes were rarely seen in town, but I couldn't stop my mind from imagining a tightly coiled rattlesnake or a long slinky python looking for a next meal down there near my feet. I didn't hear any rattling so I knew the first kind of snake wasn't in there with me and I thought a boa big enough to strangle me would be bigger than what I felt. My mind wasn't comforted but took off in further flights of fancy imagining a small dragon licking its chops and deciding what to do with me or one of those reptiles that had escaped into the sewers. Seems like there was a story about one of those pet crocodiles someone had flushed down the toilet and it grew in the sewers nearly every week in the *Inquirer*. As hard as I tried not too, I quickly convinced myself that was what had found me. I gritted my teeth and prepared for the worst. I held my frozen pose for what seemed hours ... but was probably about three minutes. Nothing happened. The lump that was at the bottom of the box grew warmer but didn't move. Without shifting too much, I lifted my head and tried to suss out what might be down there, but there wasn't enough light inside my cozy little den.

"Now, understand that the box wasn't that big. After a few minutes, I could feel more warmth coming from the creature and the shivering slowed down. Ok, so I was reasonably sure the creature was not an alligator or crocodile. Are dragons cold-blooded? Do they give off heat like mammals? I racked my brain but couldn't remember.

"The sides of the box shuddered softly again. I realized that whatever was there was leaning against the cardboard sides and shivering. Feeling a small amount of heat, I wrote off the reptiles in favor of vicious mammals. Ok, so maybe there was a small mammal of some kind ... something as cold and miserable as I was. Probably not a tiger or a bear since they would have crowded me out of the box right away, if not eaten me straight away. I shook the silly thoughts out of my head and decided, if this creature wasn't going to mess with me, I wouldn't bother it. I tried not to move a muscle and went to sleep. I reassured myself that if I lay still and left it alone, the beast would probably be gone by morning. Nights like this were long, but they did end. I must have drifted off some time later and shifted in my sleep.

"When I woke up, I was on my right side, facing the outside of the box. The sun was barely up. The light was just enough to show forms and shadows in the alley, but inside the box was still too dark. I looked down at the end of my space. I couldn't see anything there. I decided I'd either imagined the episode completely, or the thing had slithered out in the night like I hoped it would. I gave a small laugh at myself. Just as I decided to answer nature's call, I felt something beside me move. I realized my legs weren't as cold as they usually were. There was a nice warm spot in the curl of my knees. I carefully raised up as much as I could and looked down. A matted pile of hair that lay wadded up behind my legs shifted as I moved. I wasn't sure what it was until two beady eyes appeared in the middle of all that hair.

"There was fear in those liquid eyes, but also a plea. I could feel the tension in the small body, prepared to jump at the slightest provocation. I decided the plea in the eyes promised that it wouldn't hurt me if I didn't make it move. I silently agreed and decided Nature could wait a bit longer. I stretched out slightly to ease my stiffness. The instant I moved the furry pile sprang to the furthest corner of the box.

"I murmured softly and tried to assure whatever it was that I was nothing to worry about. I let myself drift off to sleep once more. While I slept, the pile crept back into the crook of my legs. When I woke the next time, the sun was full bright and the rain was gone. The warm spot had moved into the small of my back. I twisted around as carefully as I could and made sure the furry mound was the same pile of hair

I had seen earlier. The lump was still asleep. As I looked at the shaggy little body, the fur shifted and its head rose. In the next second, I realized the hairy mound was a little grey dog.

"I cautiously reached out a hand and let myself be sniffed. When that was done, I turned my hand over and gently patted the top of its head. Then, believe it or not, that damned thing smiled at me. The dog just drew its top lip back in an odd version of a smile, showing its top teeth to me.

"At first, I thought I was going to be bitten or at least growled at, but the dog stayed right there, grinning at me. I had to smile back. The pup had the ugliest set of lower teeth that stuck out I'd ever seen. But when the animal smiled, the sun seemed to get just a little brighter in the box. I turned over on my back, smiled down at the pup and carefully reached down to touch its head again. I felt the soft fur and rubbed the dog's head gently. I swear the thing sighed and snuggled in closer.

"When I finally had to get out of the box, the dog followed me. I figured out soon enough that the animal was a female so I named her Shaggy Maggie. She had short, stubby legs and an oddly long body for her size. I had no idea what breed she was. She seemed to be happy hanging around with me. When I went to the dumpster to get breakfast, Maggie followed me and sat at my feet as polite as can be. I asked her if she was hungry and she sneezed. I asked if she liked bread. She looked at me again and sneezed twice. I decided sneezing was her way of agreeing.

CHAPTER

"From that day on, she was with me everywhere I went. She made me laugh every day with her funny antics. She had a wicked sense of humor and even laughed at all my jokes. I thought she was the woman I had always wanted to live with me. Ok, so, the ones in my dreams were built a little differently but, when you are in your nineties, dreams change!

"I told Maggie everything and I swear she sometimes talked back. No, I'm not saying I heard actual voices and I don't think she could really talk to me, but saying things out loud to her made my thoughts feel more real. She looked me square in the eye and paid more attention to me than anyone ever had. She even nodded sometimes."

I looked at Frankie. He was watching me intently, like he was trying to decide whether to believe me or not. I leaned up away from the thin, worn pillows folded in behind me and whispered to the fascinated kid, "In fact, the idea to do all the things they thought I did was Maggie's. She supported me all the way and helped me plan everything."

I could tell I had his total attention now. Like a little kid wanting to hear more of a favorite tale, he leaned in and asked, "How did she do that?"

I went back against the pillows, satisfied that I had him hooked, and said, "Well then, that's the story, isn't it!"

I put on my most wistful look and told him sadly that no one had seen Maggie since I had been picked up. I sure did miss that little dog.

I looked at him with what I hoped were big sheepish, sad eyes, and said, "I hope she's getting enough to eat and had somewhere dry to live."

Then I pulled my pillows down on the cot and lay down. I closed my eyes, heaved a huge fake sigh and pretended to fall asleep. Now, I probably looked to the kid like I was sleeping, but when I look like I'm relaxing is actually when I do my best work... thinking and planning. He didn't know that so he decided to let me be.

I heard the boy call Pete to let him out and listened while they discussed how he had probably exhausted the poor old guy. I struggled not to smile. I'd been whining to Pete about Maggie since I was put in here, trying to get him to understand that she had no one else and nowhere to go. Pete told the kid that, if he could find Maggie, she could stay with me, but he wasn't using police resources to find her. If I had played my cards right, this kid would be bringing my Maggie to me and then the real story could begin. Old man indeed! We'd see who could play this game better.

Sure, enough the next day, the kid showed up. I heard him shuffling down the long echoing hall toward my little space. Pete was telling him not to make a mess and that he was holding him personally responsible. I stayed stretched out on my bunk, with my cast propped up on the end of the cot and waited till the kid was at the door. He paused. Then he cleared his throat and said he had brought me something. I stretched like I was just waking up and looked at him.

Snap! He'd done what I'd asked! There was Maggie, struggling to get out of his arm He put her down. She wiggled through the bars and rocket-launched herself into my arms I was laughing and trying to avoid being licked to death. Maggie was shaking and wiggle-wagging everything she owned. I was afraid she'd spring a leak if she didn't settle down. The kid stood over us grinning like a fool.

"I suppose," I said to the kid, "you think I owe you now, right?"

He tipped his head slightly to the right and said, "I want the story. I'm interested. You want to be famous and I want to be a real reporter. I figure we can help each other out."

I cuddled Maggie up close to my face and breathed in her hairy doggy smell. I guess I could help this kid out. He'd done this favor for me and I really couldn't complete my dream without him.

"Deal," I said. "You come back every day with food for Maggie – she likes chicken, by the way – and take her for a walk once in a while and I'll tell you my story. The whole and real truth. We'll make a book out of this thing and both end up famous."

He nodded. I asked if Maggie'd taken care of business before they came in. He nodded, "Pete said I better figure something out because he wasn't walking that dog."

I did my raised eyebrow look at him and said, "I suppose you want to start writing now."

To my surprise, he said no. He had homework to do and needed to study for a big exam the next day. Homework!!! That reminded me what a kid he was. I wondered for a minute if I was wrong to put my trust in him. But then, when you got right down to it, I didn't have much choice, did I?

He said he would be back after school tomorrow and we'd start then. I waved him off and snuggled back down to watch Maggie explore her new digs. After she finished, she jumped up on the bed and looked at me. She sneezed in approval of the new place. She walked up the length of my body and settled into the crook of my waist where she liked to lie the most. I patted her head and began to think about how I was going to tell this kid my story. How I was going to make him understand that what I'd done wasn't out of spite or malicious intent. I just needed to take care of me. Things had just gotten out of hand and the Universe had conspired against me at every turn.

CHAPTER

5

True to his word, the kid came back, but not the next day. On Saturday morning, he brought freshly cooked chicken for Maggie and ham and egg biscuits for me. He said his mom made them. I told him to thank her for me. We sat quietly and ate. I looked at the last bite of the biscuit and smiled. When the kid asked me if I was thinking about the story, I was about to tell him, I said, "No. I was just remembering something someone told me once."

He looked at me askance and I continued,

"Did you ever think that a good breakfast of ham and eggs represents just a single day's work for the chicken, but a whole lifetime for the poor pig?" I smiled broadly at him. He shook his head without even a smile and shrugged. Ok, so his sense of humor needed work. Personally, I thought the joke was kinda funny. Maybe he'd get the joke later.

Of course, Maggie finished eating first, as always. She sat down on her haunches between us, licked her lips, looked up at me and then the kid. When we didn't respond with a hand out, she sneezed several times reminding us she was there, just in case we needed help with that last bite or two. When the kid looked down at her, she stretched her top lip back and wagged her tail at him.

"Hey! She smiled!" The kid yelled. "She actually smiled at me." He laughed and pulled part of his sandwich off for her. Maggie worked her magic on him. She gently took the bite from his finger and sat back down to see if I had anything left. She was always a lady, our Maggie was.

I smiled at her working her charms and said, "I told you, she is a funny little dog, but she knows good people when she meets them. Since she likes you, I guess I will too. By the way, when she sneezes, she's telling you she agrees with you." I patted the bed and Maggie jumped up. She curled down beside me and, in no time, was snoring like a fiend. For a little dog, her snores resonated throughout the cell. The kid laughed again.

"She is pretty amazing," he said.

I patted her head and said, "You have no idea, Kid. If things go south for me, maybe you can take care of her for me." I ignored his questioning look and cleared my throat. "So, let's get started, shall we?"

I settled into my space on the cot, plumping up my pillows and resting my cast on the end of the bed. With theatrical grace, I cleared my throat and said, "Everything started about a year ago. I'd scraped enough money from gathering cans and bottles to buy a couple beers at my favorite old haunt.

"I liked spending time with the guys I'd known for years. It didn't happen often anymore, but money in my pocket made me feel like a man again. Several of my old drinking buddies called me by name when I came in the door. Most of them were younger than me and still working, but they accepted me as a part of the little party whenever I showed up. We spent the evening chatting like guys do about what they'd do if they won the lottery, making up lies about women they claimed to have known in their lives, and complaining about how hard they'd to work for so little money. When my first beer ran dry, one of the guys always bought me a second round. They all realized how little cash I had and felt sorry for me. But I didn't care ... pity beer goes down just as well as bought beer!

"One of the guys said he heard the town was going to do something special for the oldest person living here on the 100th anniversary of the town's founding. Another one said he had read about the plan in the paper. His crazy old aunt was all excited because she was close to being the oldest person in town. She read about the prize, called him up and made him take her down to register as described in the article. She came out with less enthusiasm than she went in, as the official had told her there were at least a dozen people in town older than her.

"I asked who his aunt was. He told me and I said, 'Hell, she was a grade younger than me in elementary school.'

"One of them nudged me and asked how old I was. When I told him, he said, 'You are right up there, buddy.'

"'What's the big prize?' I asked. He explained that the oldest person in town on the anniversary day would get free housing, free medical, free food for life and $50,000 cash.'

The kid looked up and said, "Wow."

"I know," I countered and continued.

"I didn't believe him, so I waved my hand and pshawed him. That had to be drunk talk. I said that had to be a lie because this town was tighter than a jar of peanut butter at a squirrel convention. One guy started laughing and said, 'Well, think about what she said, Scabby.'

Another nodded into his beer and said, 'If he's old enough, he'd sure as hell better try.'

"All the guys started laughing and talking about how I ought to go down to the courthouse and fill out the forms being as old as I was. Who knew? One of them added, 'Besides, I bet the town figures whoever wins won't be around long enough to cost them that much money.'

"With that, the whole table erupted. They started cracking old folk's jokes at my expense. I figured that the free beer had come to an end, so I left the table with jeers and catcalls trailing behind me.

"Young punks! They just didn't know yet how much being old changed everything, but I did. The idea of living the rest of my life in a warm, furnished real house with real cooked food, someone to fix my bunions, a cozy place to sleep every night and money to spend rather than living out my time in my leaky old box, sick and broke … well, even six months would be worth whatever it took to win!

"That night, curled up in our box, I told Maggie all about what I had heard. She listened with rapt attention, her curly head on my chest and ears perked. When I asked her what she thought, she sat up and seemed to think for a few minutes. Then she sneezed two quick little bobs of her head, curled her upper lip into a winning smile and then cuddled back down. I guess that was her way of saying, 'Hell, man what are you waiting for? Free chicken for the rest of our lives?

That's what I'm talking about.'

"I started laughing at the idea of her being so happy. At the sound of my laugh, she crawled up on my chest and started licking my face. That made me laugh even harder. The more I laughed the more she wiggled and waggled her shaggy flag of a tail until she fell right off me. 'Ok, ok,' I told her, rubbing her furry sides as she curled up into the crook of my arm again. 'Tomorrow, we'll go check the information out.' She gave a contented sigh.

"I couldn't fall asleep that easy. My mind raced as I thought of the potential. If I could find out how many people were on the list ahead of me, and if I could discover their weaknesses, I might be able to help my cause along. Of course, I truly hoped I was already the oldest person alive. But a man had to have an alternate plan."

I took a look at the kid while he typed. He was smiling and nodding his head as he documented every statement. I paused to give him a few minutes to catch up. I wanted to be certain he was getting every thought down just like I said the words. When he looked up, I continued.

"As soon as the sun was up, I went down to the old Chevron gas station on the corner. I had gone to school with the owner's dad. I helped clean up around there whenever he needed it and, in return, he let me use the washroom to get all gussied up for rare important occasions. I washed up the best I could, combed my few remaining hairs and even cleaned my shoes up a bit. Then Maggie and I walked the five blocks down Elm Street to the courthouse. On the way, I talked to her about the idea I had come up with in the night. Talking to her helped wrap my own head around the idea.

"All the way there, she walked right beside me with her tail flagging high and her head up. She looked like she was proud of us. I could tell just by her prancing walk that she believed we had a good chance at winning this thing.

"When we arrived, we climbed the long stairway and stopped outside the dark oaken doors. I told her to her sit on the marble steps outside the courthouse while I went in. I gotta tell you I was a bit nervous, but when I looked back out at her, she wagged her tail and sneezed like she was telling me to get on with the job I came to do. I did.

"There was a young guy – by young, I mean about 60 – at the tall ancient counter. He looked up and, without smiling, said he figured I'd show up soon. I knit my brows and looked at him. He scoffed a little and said that I did not know him, but he sure knew me. He told me his grandmother was Mary Jane Sweetly. He said his grandmother still talked about how cute Scabby Loudon was and how she was going to marry him someday. I tried to look sorry and dropped my head a bit. He said not to worry. She was in a nursing home, completely out of her mind with Alzheimer's. She thought she was seven years old. He said she talked about me so much that he had asked around about me. When people pointed me out and he saw who I was, he said he just didn't get the attraction. He leaned on the polished counter and cupped his chin in his hands. Then he asked, "What could she have possibly seen in you?"

"I smiled and told him, "Well, I was a much taller, more handsome guy back in second grade."

"He smiled a bit then and seemed to let me off the hook a little. He asked what he could do for me in a bit warmer tone than he'd greeted me with. I told him what I'd heard and he confirmed the story. He even said he was glad I had come in. By his reckoning, there were only six people who had a solid chance at winning the prize and I was one of them. I was pretty surprised. He saw the look in my eyes and told me how all contenders were about the same age. But only the one who was the oldest and was still alive in eleven months, when the drawing would be held, would win the grand prize. He handed me a sheet of pale-yellow paper. He stood staring at me as I looked at the form. This could not be this easy.

"'So, let me get this straight,' I said to him. 'All I have to do is be the oldest person alive in this town when the centennial hits?'

"Yup, that's the plan," he said.

"And there are only six of us in the running?" He nodded his head.

"'Funny enough," he said, "I did some digging. You all would have been in the same graduating class in high school ... if you had stayed in school.'

"I curled my lip up into my best Elvis sneer impersonation at that dig. I really didn't need to be reminded that I'd never graduated. 'Can you tell me who they are,' I asked.

"He shook his head. 'That wouldn't be right. We wouldn't want anyone doing anything unfair, now would we?' I must have looked at him oddly because he laughed and said, 'Seriously, we'll be printing the names of those who registered in the paper on Sunday. Then everyone will know who the contenders are.'

"Filling out the papers didn't require much effort -- birthdate, full name, residence. I finished the exercise quickly.

"'Seems a little ghoulish to me,' I said as I finished filling out the form. I pushed the page back to him. 'I mean, there'll be five of us out there, all hoping like hell the others kick the bucket before we do.'

"His brows lifted at that idea. He gathered up the paper and said in a priggish voice, 'Well Mr. Loudon, I doubt anyone else would think of that. *They*' – he emphasized that word – 'are all good Christian people.' He left the words 'unlike you who I never see in church' silent. I struggled not to let lose my inner five-year-old who wanted to wrinkle up his nose and stick his tongue out at him. With a superior look down his nose, he picked the paper up and turned his back on me.

"I tried to stop words from coming out, I swear I did, but the words just leaped from my lips. 'Like hell,' I said, 'we all will be praying for the others to move on – in one way or another.' I turned on my worn-down heels, threw back my shoulders, and walked out the door in as dignified a manner as I could.

"To the casual observer, I looked calm and steady but, on the inside, my head was spinning a bit at the idea of what could happen as I stepped out into the sunshine again. Maggie was still on the steps, as I knew she would be. I plopped down heavily. She looked at me with concerned eyes and waited. When I steadied my mind and nerves, I put my hand out and rubbed Maggie's skinny back as I explained what had happened inside. She listened quietly until I finished. That's when she made me realize we could win this thing. She jumped to her feet and raced around me barking, turning in circles, and wiggling until I stood up. She pranced down the street, with her tail beckoning me to follow. Now, some people might think she was just headed toward the diner to see if there was any chicken in the dumpster like we usually did at this time every day. But, when she dropped her little fanny on the sidewalk right in front of the library and scratched her ears, I knew exactly what she wanted us to do.

"I grabbed her up and hugged her. We walked on to the diner. I went inside and bought us some freshly cooked chicken with the last of my beer money. We sat on the curb and ate. I let her lick my fingers while I explained, in soft tones so no one walking by overheard me ... not that anyone ever paid attention to a dirty old homeless man talking to a scruffy little dog. I detailed what we needed to do, and she listened intently until the chicken ran out. While I cleaned up the area, Maggie disappeared around the corner of the building. When she came back, we headed back toward the public library to do some research."

I looked up at the kid. He'd been very quiet the whole time. Just jotting a few notes down when he needed to. I could tell he was still interested. I asked him, "What would you have done in my place."

He shrugged.

I said, "I'll tell you. You would have done just what I did."

"I left Maggie on the front steps of the library and went in. They knew me well there. The same librarians appeared to have been there as long as I'd been alive, though I probably just imagined that. There must have been quite a few different ones over time, but they all seemed to have the same prim and proper look, Lily of the Valley scent and patient demeanor. I had to admit some of the younger ones were changing the traditional librarian mode. For instance, the room wasn't as quiet as I remembered in my youth. No one enforced the "shhh rule" like they used to do. People were less considerate of the space than in generations past, but the place was still a refuge for me. Change seemed slow in this industry.

"I walked over to the reference desk and asked if I could see the annual for what would have been my senior year of high school. I stood quietly while Miss Adams, who had been working there for at least ten years and knew me well, acted like I was a stranger and might not be trustable with such an important item. Finally, after a long moment, she went to retrieve the book. When she returned, she held the volume to her chest like an infant she was about to part with for the first time. I gave her my brightest smile and told her I knew the routine. I had already washed my hands – I even showed them to her -- and I would stay right here at the table by her desk. She hesitated only a moment longer, then returned my smile, and handed over the treasured bit of memorabilia. She reminded me that the book was an irreplaceable part of the town's history. I didn't remind her that I'd never hurt a book and I'd always returned things right away. I promised to sit right there at the table next to her desk and look at the photos. I didn't even mention that I happened to know there were at least thirty copies of the exact same book in the back. I just smiled. I told you this town was tight!

"I turned to the table and pulled the closest chair back gently and sat down. When I opened the musty-smelling book, the pages fell open and memories came roaring out. All those young bright faces were hard to look at as they smiled up at me expectantly. They each looked like they had a great future ahead of them and yet, no matter what they'd accomplished or gained, many of them were worm food now. I found the page that held photos of what would have been my graduating class. Forty-two faces, some more familiar than others, but all known. I went through, ticking off the ones who had died. There were several who'd been soldiers in the various wars who'd died serving their country. I mentally saluted them, including John Talley who I knew to be a massive jerk, even in kindergarten. I wondered what had become of his browbeaten wife and kids. I saw Janie Dupree who'd lost her life, giving birth to her ninth child. I briefly wondered what had happened to that brood. Then I saw the inseparable Macksin twins who had died within hours of each other at the age of 75 from unknown illnesses. So many were gone. I tried to ignore the feeling of loss as I went through the list and wrote down the names of my competition."

Back to reality, I rubbed my hand over my eyes. The memories were tiring. I told the kid that he had to go. I needed to sleep. He asked if I wanted him to take Maggie out. I told him no, I needed her with me. I turned to face the wall and felt Maggie slide into her place under my chin. She made me feel better as I drifted off to sleep.

CHAPTER

The kid didn't come back on Sunday. Can't say as I blamed him. I'm sure a kid his age has a lot to do on a weekend. If I had been him, I'd been sleeping off a good party. Or hanging around with some girl who didn't want me to go home yet. But I didn't get the feeling that this kid was like that. Naw, he was probably doing homework.

I thought about the times when Maggie and I sat on the bed made of newspaper in our box and planned our caper. I thought about the competition and wondered how this was going to end. I needed to find out some more stuff about each one. I was fairly certain that the list I made would match the list in the paper. This town was not a place people moved to. No one new had moved here for years. And, if they had, the town busy-body word-of-mouth communication system would have notified everyone. That's one of the most standard things about little towns. No one has secrets in a small town. Never move to one if you have something to hide. Soon enough, everyone will know.

Of course, with me, everyone knew about my secrets until recently. They had lived through most of them with me. I've always been pretty much an open book. If there was a secret about me, then you can be pretty well guaranteed I didn't know the story either. I read somewhere that you should never expect another person to keep your secret. After all, if you can't keep the secret, why should anyone else? So, I never tried to keep any. No sense putting undue pressure on anyone ... especially me.

Now, I sat in the jail and thought about the days not so long ago when I was trying to put together a plan to assure my winning the prize. Maggie was a great help. The way she looked at me made me think I could do anything. "If we make this happen," I used to tell her, "You'll be having hot chicken every day and a warm soft bed." She always sneezed in agreement and lay down beside me. I'd rub her head a bit and drift off to sleep alongside her.

Almost Brilliant

CHAPTER

Monday after school, the kid showed up with a laptop. He said he had talked to the editor of the paper and they were interested in doing a longer story, but only if I'd get the story told before the trial and the verdict. I told him we'd get the job done. The kid set up the computer and waited for me to start.

I told him, "Before we get started, I decided I'll tell you a story a day until we get to how I got here. But here I have one demand, a non-negotiable demand."

The kid about broke his neck, whipping around to look at me. He gulped and nodded. I said, "In the most serious voice I could muster, you can't tell anyone what we talk about till after the trial is over. You gotta swear or I'm not saying another word."

He looked at me sadly and said, "What about my editor? He wants to know what I'm doing. He even loaned me this laptop so he wouldn't have to try to read my handwriting."

I asked, "Is he paying you?"

The kid dropped his head. He shook his head from side to side and his hair looked like sea kelp waving back and forth in an underwater tide pool.

"Ok then," I whispered conspiratorially, "tell him you are working on a story and it's big. Keep him interested but don't tell him too much. And don't tell the sheriff anything either! Agreed?"

"I gave up fighting my inner demons a long time ago. We're pretty much on the same side now. As I looked at that fresh young kid, I could almost see the good little angel and the bad little devil jumping up and down on his shoulders as he tried to decide what to do. I doubted he was used to keeping secrets of any kind from anyone. After a few minutes, the bad little devil must've knocked the angel's wings into the dirt and the kid nodded in agreement.

"'So, what exactly are you going to tell me,' he asked. 'Are you going to tell me why you started this?' This kid was an airhead. He still didn't get my meaning.

"'Listen to me, Kid,' I said, 'if you were given the choice of living out the rest of your days in a cold wet cardboard box while your neighbors relieved themselves nearby and scrounging for every meal, or living in a real house with all your needs taken care of, what would you do?"

The kid bobbed his head like one of the dolls in the back window of a car as he chewed on that idea.

Then he said he'd thought of another question

he wanted to ask me. I looked at him and waited for the question. He asked, "What made you think you could actually get away with killing all these people in the first place?"

"First," I said, "get this through your thick head and you need to keep this thought in the front of your mind at all times. I never planned to kill anyone nor did I actually kill anyone. I was just going to help them along to their just rewards. I was being helpful and kind."

He ducked his head, but not before I saw his eyes narrow and his lips purse in obvious disbelief."

"Second, Maggie," I said. "She supported every idea."

"He shook his head without looking up.

"I held up a hand and said, "Not point blank by telling me what to do, mind you, but by doing things that made me feel like I was on the right path."

"For instance, the night after making the list, when I was settling down for the night, Maggie suddenly left the box. That surprised me because she always climbed in with me and never left my side during the night. She was gone for a few minutes. I was just beginning to wonder about her when she trotted in, scampered up the length of me, and dropped something on my chest. I picked up a damp, furry pile and half turned toward the front of the box where the light was better. There in my hand was a dead mouse. Maggie sat right there in the middle of my chest and looked at the mouse. Then looked back and forth between me and the furry mess three or four times.

"Of course, I threw the carcass away. Maggie snorted and went to the bottom of the box instead of snuggling in beside me. I thought about her gift for a long time after I heard her snores echoing around the box. Long about dawn, I figured out what the dead mouse meant. She gave me the idea to get rid of the others. I mean, she went out and killed a gift for me, the least I could do was give her a gift back, right? That's when the plan really started to take shape, but then everyone knows the road to success is always under construction. I still had a lot of planning and work to do.

"After the trip to the library and that gift," I told him, "Maggie and I did a lot of research trying to decide what to do. I thought briefly about trying to become the oldest person in the whole country. With the help of one of the young library aides, I did a Google search on the topic. Did you know there are over 72,000 people in this country over 100 years old? I guess trying to set a Guinness book record of being the oldest person in the United States would be too tough. If I was going to make a mark in history, I guess that mark had to be made here.

"I looked at the other people that were competing and they were already comfortably off – not a single one was homeless like me – but they all had health problems I was the only one who needed to win. So, I decided to, shall we say, assist Nature and remove my competition."

"You really were going to kill them?" The kid's voice went up about six octaves. The shock in his face was glorious. This kid was too easy!

"No, I told you. I just wanted to help Nature along. Each one of them had a medical complication. I just wanted to help ease them on their way a bit. They were all nice people. They just didn't need to suffer like they were, you know. I felt like helping them was the least I could do to save them from any extra suffering."

The kid shook his head. I could tell he was struggling with the idea. "Before you get all huffy about this, Kid, you just wait till I tell you the whole story. And, remember, I'm the victim here. Not those people."

"The first one," I said, "on the list was Creed Remington, or as I knew him from grade school, SnotGun."

The kid looked at me and asked if the nickname

was because of his last name. I shook my head.

"Much better than that," I said. "In second grade, we were doing an art project with watercolors. SnotGun was always sniffing and snuffing his nose. That kid had a cold or something all the time. His nose never stopped running. He was always wiping snot on his shirt sleeves, even though he had wads of tissue in his pockets and his desk. Nothing seemed to stop his drippy nose or kept him from sneezing.

"Anyway, we were all hard at work. The teacher had just patted him on the back and told him what a nice artistic piece he was doing. Without looking up, he said thank you and then drew back and sneezed so hard that a huge wad of snot flew out of his nose and landed dead center in the middle of the page. I am talking huge!"

The kid turned a bit green, but I kept on with the story.

"One of the other kids said that that snot came out and splatted like a gunshot. Someone else laughed and called his sneeze a 'gun snot'. That's how he got the nickname. We all laughed at that and started calling him that name from then on, no matter how hard the teacher tried to make us stop. The name was just too funny and appropriate for us to get past."

The kid shook his head and kept typing.

"I know, that's gross. You know that he became the richest man in the area, right? Well, to look at Mr. I'm-so-rich-now Banker in his three hundred-dollar suits and his Italian leather shoes, you'd never think of him with that name."

To his credit, the kid chuckled a bit at the idea of calling the richest guy in the area by that childish nickname.

"Yeah," I continued, "that was a good one. Anyway, in middle school, they figured out he had allergies and fixed the problem, but he never lived down the name. Even when his daddy died and left him in charge of the bank, those of us who knew him still called him SnotGun. Not to his face if we needed a loan or anything but definitely behind his back."

"Fact is old SnotGun was the source of a lot of the best times of my life. He hired me a lot when I was in my working prime. Yeah, he owned a lot of companies who hired day laborers. There was always yard work or some kind of grunt job that needed to be done. And I could always count on him to get me to my next party. On Friday nights he'd always bring cases of cold beer to the work sites and get the weekend started right. We all loved him for that."

I shook my head and continued by saying, "Even though he'd been sort of good to me at times in my life, he was in my way now. He didn't need to win this competition. He already had a fine house and all the money he'd ever need plus some. He had no family so he had probably already left his money to some charity, maybe the school system. They could always use the money. He was laying up there all alone in that big old house with a ticker that was threatening to go any day now anyway. The way I figured, not only would I be helping him on his way to his final resting place, but I'd be helping the future generations as well. So, you see, I was not putting my needs first."

The kid smiled and typed a few more notes.

I continued on. "A few days later, Maggie and I were sitting on the bench outside the diner when I heard that SnotGun was in the hospital after another attack from his bad ticker. He was being released that day and he'd to hire a nurse to be with him because he refused to stay in the hospital."

The kid raised an eyebrow in question.

"Don't tell me," he said, "you have some nursing skills."

"Don't be daft," I snapped. "I ain't no nurse. Though that would have made things a lot easier."

"So, what was the plan," asked the kid.

"Well," I reached out and patted Maggie's

head. "I got the idea from Maggie here." Up went those bushy eyebrows again. "I'm telling you, every time I needed an idea, she came up with a good one."

"I was feeling like I needed a little social interaction so I went down to the place by the river where all the homeless guys hung out. In the summer, we all just lay around on the grass under the trees. When the weather turned cold, we lit a fire, shared whatever booze we had and told lies about our younger lives. We all knew we were lying, but no one cared. The storytelling passed the time. And time passed faster when the stories were larger than life.

"One guy started talking about a woman he heard about in the next town over. She was a real stripper. He said she dressed up like a nurse and took every little stitch of clothes off. We all gasped at that. Though we would never have admitted the truth, none of us had ever actually seen a live stripper. We egged the guy on to tell us more about her. "Yeah," he said, loving that he had an audience, "she's working over at Barney's. Not that young but still pretty – with a decent figure." He said she used to work in New York or somewhere. She came here because her mother used to live here."

"They all started muttering and making up stories about strippers they had seen and the weird things they would do. Pack of liars.

"The only person I could think of that had ever left town was Marcia Marie Hemming. If you remember, we were sweethearts in grade school but I lost track of her after I left school early. I think I was about 40 when we started up again. She was a year or two younger than me. I was practically living with her until one day, after I came back from a week-long construction job out of town. I went to the house we shared and she was gone. Just up and left. No one could tell me what happened. The waitress at the Blue Diamond café, who knew everyone and everything, said she left for the big city and was never coming back.

"That must have been sad for you," the kid said.

I tipped my head slightly to the right and smiled a bit. "Probably was for the best. She was getting a bit clingy. Before I left, I had caught her crying a couple times and, when I asked what was up, she said nothing. I really don't like weeping females. So, I had pretty much decided that our time together was over anyway." I shrugged off that memory. A crazy thought had crossed my mind at the time but, well, you know how it is – guys sow their wild oats and then pray for crop failure. We'd sown a lot of oats together but I figured she'd have told me if there was anything important I needed to know.

"So, back to SnotGun. There he was all sick and alone. One afternoon, I figured I'd go pay my respects. I went up there to that huge old house and knocked on the door, big as you please. A tall, dour woman in a white uniform pulled the heavy oak door open and looked at me with a cautious smile on her face. The smile was quickly replaced with a hard look that made me think I had stepped in something as I walked over the lawn. I promise you, her nose tipped up so high that I doubt she could see me below her. I realized that I wasn't the best-dressed person in the world, but I had cleaned up. I told her I was there to see my friend, Mr. Remington. She looked at me like I was a stray on the porch, sniffed and said he was far too ill to have visitors. I should come back some other day and I should call to make an appointment first. Before I could tell her, I didn't have a phone, she closed the door in my face none too lightly. I watched through the foyer windows as she tromped across the hallway and into the library. I'd been in that house so many times as a kid for parties, and later to drink illegally that I knew the layout as well as anyone.

"I slipped around the side of the house, through the bushes and went in through the semi-hidden cellar door. I took the back stairs that were hidden in the walls of the mansion and went up to the master bedroom. Even though the long undisturbed dust was thick enough to show the entry hadn't been used for a long while, the big old door didn't complain when I pulled the heavy wood open. On the other side of the room lay SnotGun on his big fancy bed. He had what seemed like a hundred pillows all around him and tubes and wires running all over the place. In the corner at the head of the bed was white metal machine that beeped softly every second. Squiggly lines ran evenly across the monitor.

"When I got to the end of the bed, I touched his foot softly. The monitor gave a soft beep and one of the lines jumped around a bit as he opened his eyes and looked at me. Took him a second to recognize me, but then he smiled. The monitor settled back into its steady rhythm.

"Hey Snotty," I half whispered. "I came to see how you are. Heard you were under the weather." He just smiled. I continued, "I thought you could use some cheering up so I slipped past that jailor you have working for you and came in the secret way."

He smiled and said, "She's too good at her job."

I sat on his bed for a while and we chatted about old times. When we got to new times, I asked real casual like if he'd heard about the oldest person thing. He had. In fact, he said that he put up the cash prize part. In my head, that helped me realize that what I was planning to do was even more right. Putting up the money for his own prize was just wrong for a man to do!

"When I heard the nurse's heavy step on the stairs, I told him I'd better go. I told him I'd be back to visit again soon. He smiled, nodded and closed his eyes. I slipped out the hidden door to the staircase just as the nurse came in. Then, just as big as you please, I walked into the main part of the house through the library and right out that front door and down the drive! No stuffy nurse was going to tell me where I could and couldn't go.

The kid smiled and kept typing.

"How are you doing? Keeping up?" I asked in mock concern. He nodded and lifted his fingers. Flexing them, he said that typing was a lot easier than writing.

I smiled and said, "Well hang on 'cause here is where the story gets good."

"The following Thursday night I was down by the river with the guys again. After the initial conversation lagged, one of them took a deep swig from the community jug and said how he'd been thinking about that stripper and how he'd like to go see her. You know, just to see if what he heard was all true or not. A couple of the guys said casually that they wouldn't mind tagging along. Next thing I knew, somebody was going to borrow their brother's car. We agreed to pool our money for gas and drive over to check her out the next night.

"I walked home with a nice little buzz and curled up in my box. Maggie was waiting for me like usual. I told her how I was gonna be gone the next night and she'd have to stay here and wait for me to get back. She licked my hand and snuggled in for the night. I drifted off thinking of better-than-thou nurses, lovely naked strippers and poor old SnotGun. Somewhere in the night, a stunningly brilliant idea hit me. I sat bolt upright and knocked my head on the top of the box. Maggie jumped up from a dead sleep and bounced out onto the asphalt. I bet she thought we were being attacked or something. She stood all stiff-legged, looking around for the enemy. I reached out, patted her head to calm her down and told her what woke me up. She dropped her butt on the ground and sat staring at me for a few seconds, like she was mulling the idea over. Then she gave that little sneeze that I knew meant she approved of my plan and crawled back into her place. I tried to go back to sleep, but this idea was too perfect.

"The next night, five of us pooled our money to buy gas and drove over to Barney's. We walked in as a group, trying to be nonchalant, but we were more excited than kids at our first circus. We'd all cleaned up for the trip with fresh clothes and a shave. Of course, some of us were cleaner than the others. Personally, I'd borrowed some clothes from a house where I knew they liked to hang clothes outside to dry. Not many people did that anymore.

The kid looked at me in askance.

"Now before you get all judgmental," I told him. "The dirty clothes I'd been wearing had come from the same place and I left them there – a fair trade. I was doing the right thing by returning the old things." I smiled slyly and winked. He just shook his head and went back to typing.

"Like I said," I continued, we had agreed that

we'd pool the rest of our money after we bought the gas and only drink beer. We weren't there to get drunk or get into trouble of any kind. We just wanted to see the stripper. We arrived about an hour early, which gave us enough time to drink the edge off before her show. Even though we didn't expect anything big to happen, we all hoped we'd have great stories to tell the others who didn't come with us the night. I bet the other guys were already thinking up lies before we even got there, but I was there for a different reason.

"Just about the time those good old boys were starting to get really relaxed and bragging again, the lights in the far corner of the room brightened. A makeshift stage had been created by putting an old piece of plywood on top of several beer kegs. In the middle of the stage was a tether ball pole with some sad looking ribbons hanging from the rusted ball at the top. That pole didn't look capable of holding a little kid let alone an adult stripper, but who am I to judge? Off to one side, someone had hung a large shimmery purple curtain that had been hung across the far corner and attached the cloth to one of the other dirty old walls in some unclear manner.

CHAPTER

8

"A recorded fanfare announced the arrival of the owner of the place. Barney himself stepped up with a karaoke mic in his hand. Immediately, the audience started catcalling for him to get off the stage and bring on the dancer, but Barney felt the need to tell us the rules. He signaled to the bartender and tapped the head of the mic to be sure the amp was on. Despite the mic in his hand, he screamed at the men.

"'I'm not starting the show, he said, until you hooligans understand the rules. You get me?'

There was a rattle of jeers from the back of the room, but the twenty plus men quieted down.

"'I want you to understand this is a nice place,' he demanded, 'and we don't want any trouble. There will be no touching of the dancer. No one will try to grab her – in fact, you barbarians better stay on the other side of the rail.' He indicated two extra kegs with a rope tied around them and stretched out in front of the stage. 'Definitely no fighting. Anyone who starts a fight for any reason is out.'

"He said she may be a working girl, but she was just trying to earn a living just like anyone else and we should behave. That brought on a smattering of jeers from around the room, but they were quickly silenced. He ended his speech by pointing to a large bearded man sitting on a stool next to the stage. He may have been intimidating at one stage in his life but now, well, let's just say he hadn't been in the gym for a long while.

"'If these rules are ignored,' he yelled, 'you'll

be talking to my man over here.' There were a few snickers but no one outright laughed. He may not have looked that fit, but we all knew from experience what could happen when a guy that size got his meat hooks on you.

"Personally," I said to the kid, "I think Barney was far more worried about cops showing up than that girl's feelings getting hurt or anything. In that part of the county, cops wouldn't show up unless there was a ruckus of some kind so he was just covering his backside and making the whole speech sound like he was all caring and stuff. Most of us chuckled into our beer glasses and yelled for him to get off the stage.

"Finally, he was done talking and stepped into the shadows. The lights went down. From the speaker, we heard ... 'and now, gentlemen, direct from New York City, here she is, the one, the only, LouLou von Sugartown!' Another scratchy song with lots of bass blared out over the old loudspeaker. I didn't recognize the melody, but then I didn't care either. At the back of the so-called stage, the enormous shimmering purple cloth shivered and a white nylon clad leg appeared from a split in the middle. A pink spotlight flashed and the dancer slinked into view. Men started banging their beer mugs on the table, stamping their feet and hooting. The whole thing reminded me of what Marcia had once told me. She thought most women would rather have beauty than brains. When I asked her what she meant, she said, in her experience, most guys could see better than they could think. I had to give her that one! These guys were animals.

"One thing for sure, Barney was wrong to call her a girl. She was pretty enough and had a decent figure, but she had to be 40 if she was a day. Of course, because of certain, shall we say, chest high attributes and because I was there for a different reason than the others, I was probably the only one who noticed her age. All the guys were cheering and hooting. She stood there dressed in a crisp starched nurse's uniform complete with hat on her slightly frizzy blond hair and a stethoscope around her neck. Except for the ridiculously high stiletto heels, she looked like a real nurse. With a flourish, she discarded her hat and began to dance around the stage in time to the music. Piece by piece, she took each item of clothing off until she was down to her all-togethers, which could barely be called underwear. She reached both arms behind her like she was going to unleash her impressive attributes ... she paused and smiled ... the audience waited as silent as a kid waiting to see Santa come down the chimney ... and just as she loosened the clasp to show us glory, the harsh house lights came up. That cussed old Barney came running up on the stage carrying a small pink blanket. He snatched the blanket up in front of the dancer and drew the cloth around her tightly.

"The guys jumped to their feet, started screaming and banging the beer mugs on the tabletop. She stood there, smiling apologetically and shifting her weight back and forth on those ridiculous shoes nervously. Barney stood in front of her with his palms out, trying to calm the crowd. The big guy stood up, trying to look menacing. I have to say the effect was ruined by the heavily stained drop cloth tucked under his chin and the bits of fried chicken decorating his scraggly beard. I sat quietly in my chair, ready to get out the door if the crowd rushed onto the stage.

When the crowd finally shut up enough for him to talk, Barney sneered at them and told them they couldn't expect to see everything without a cover charge. He said that the real show would commence in an hour. Anyone who wanted to stay would have to leave and have to pay a $20 cover charge to get back in. The crowd roared its disapproval as he backed to the edge of the stage nearest the bar with the stripper behind him but, rather than being scared, she was waving her fingers at members of the audience and even throwing kisses. One of the guys said he was sure she didn't want to leave, which caused more angry murmurings in the crowd, but every one of the surly drunks stood up and moved to the door. By the sound of the grumbling, Barney hadn't made many friends tonight and not many were prepared to come back.

I looked up at the kid. Oh yeah, he was definitely paying attention. "Did you stay?" he asked. "Did she really take everything off?"

"How the hell would I know," I scoffed. "I left them in the parking lot counting money and trying to figure out if they could stay. But no one had $20 to pay the charge. Hell, we had used all our money for gas and the three pitchers of beer we had nursed all evening. No, we didn't stay. Well, they didn't. They'd swilled up the rest of the beer and gone back to the car grumbling and grousing about getting ripped off. I'd slipped away and let them leave, so I could stick around and wait out back until closing time. I kinda felt sorry for the woman because only about ten greasy, dirty looking guys went back in. Knowing how little money she'd make that night had made me more optimistic that she might be interested in my idea.

"I crouched in a dark corner of the parking lot just out of the light and waited for her to come out the back door. I had sat there for about thirty minutes when I realized a flaw in my otherwise well-thought-out plan. How long would the walk back take me if she didn't agree to help me out? I was kicking myself for a fool for the hundredth time, when she finally appeared. I was pleased to see she was alone. Dressed in a sweater, old jeans and far more sensible shoes, she stopped just outside the door to light a cigarette, took a deep pull and then blew the smoke out in a ring shape. Over her arm was an enormous purse that could have easily doubled as a suitcase. My guess was that she had all of her performance props in that bag. She walked toward a beat-up old Ford that had seen better days – much like its owner.

I slowly stood up, shook the creaks out of my old legs and wandered toward her trying to appear as non-menacing as I could in the empty parking lot. When I was still safely a few feet away, I called out to her. She whipped around and crouched down like a fighter, her huge purse scattering at her feet. Her hands were up at chest height, clenching something long and dark. I was hoping the dark shape wasn't a gun. She yelled at me to stay where I was. I stepped forward so I was more in the glow of the streetlight before I obeyed her command. When she saw I was an old guy, she relaxed.

'"Oh hell, you scared the crap out of me,' she snapped. I held my hands up, apologized and took a step closer. She asked what I wanted as she stooped to pick up the scattered items and cigarette she had dropped. The glare of the streetlight made her look even older and more exhausted. Without the heavy stage make-up, the wrinkles and worry lines on her face stood out as clearly as the scraps and dents on her old car.

"I told her I'd driven over from a neighboring town and told her I'd enjoyed the first show. She scoffed and asked, 'Well, did you come back for the second show?' I shook my head and said, 'I couldn't afford to come back in, but I'd wanted to'. She lifted a brow. I raised my hands palms toward her and said, 'I wanted to but not for the reasons you think.'

"She put her hands on her hips and sneered, 'What I ain't good enough for you? I'll have you know I've danced in some pretty famous places and was even in a real movie once.'

"I assured her that I had no doubt of that. She stood up and started fishing in her pants pocket. I watched as she finally pulled her keys out and unlocked the rusted car.

"'Well, if you're looking to get lucky, you lost out. I'm leaving here now ... alone.'

"She opened the squeaking door, slipped in and waved her fingertips at me. Before she could slam the door, I stepped up and put my hand on the inside of the window. She glared at me. "I thought I made my meaning clear,' she said, 'that I am leaving here ... alone.'

"'Look,' I said taking my hand off the cold glass, 'I have an idea that I need your help with ... if you're interested.' She shook her head without looking at me. 'I don't do freebies.'

"'No, no, listen,' I pleaded. 'I've just about enough money to buy a couple cups of coffee. There is an all-night diner just down the street. Can I buy you a cup and explain?' She hesitated. 'Can't you just give me that much time?' I pleaded.

"She turned the ignition, waited for the car to stop coughing and finally catch. Then she looked up at me, seemed to give the idea a bit more thought and then said she didn't drink coffee, but would love a cold drink. Then she said, 'Get in and closed the car door.' I all but scampered around before she could change her mind, glad that she decided I was as harmless as I really was.

I looked at the kid again and paused ... for effect, you know. That kid was on the edge of his seat. He wasn't even typing any more. He was leaning so far forward that I was worried he'd fall off the chair. Behind the owl glasses, his eyes were wide and his lower jaw was hanging loose.

"Better pull up that lip, kid. You'll draw flies in here." I laughed at him. He sat upright and snapped his jaw shut. He reached up and casually wiped a bit of spit off his chin and then wiped the moisture on his pant leg.

"I can't believe she agreed to go home with you," he gasped.

"No, kid," I clarified, "we just went out for coffee. But, when she heard my story, she got so interested that she ended up buying me breakfast. We talked till after the dawn."

"Go on," he said "Go on!"

I held up a hand to stop his enthusiasm. "Hold your horses. Maggie is telling me she needs to go out and I need a coffee break myself. You take

Maggie out for a stretch and I'll go make a new pot of coffee." He reluctantly stood up, grabbed the leash, walked to the door and swung the entryway open. When she saw the leash, Maggie didn't even bother with the door. She jumped off the cot, slipped out between the bars and stood waiting for him, tail wagging.

As they walked down the hall, I looked over at what he had typed. I guess the marks were some kind of shorthand because there were just words here and there. I shook my head. He'd better get this right!

Pete looked up when I walked into the breakroom to make coffee. I told you – small town jails are great.

"You telling that kid a bunch of lies in there," he asked with a twinkle in his eye.

"I sure am," I smiled back. "You know I ain't gonna tell him anything that will get me in trouble till after the trial. But, at least, I get some company this way and he thinks he's on his way to something big."

Pete just shook his head and returned to his never-ending paperwork. Good thing he didn't know what I was really doing. I didn't need any of this to come out too soon.

When the kid got back, he said he had to go. He hadn't realized how late the hour was. I didn't even ask when he was coming back. I could tell he was hooked and would return as soon as he could. Since this was Wednesday, I figured he would show up late tomorrow after school.

To my surprise, he was at the cell door, whispering my name before I had even had breakfast the next morning. In his hand, he had a bag with greasy spots and big red letters on the outside. Donuts! From the bakery I lived behind! I kinda missed those donuts. Even though I usually got the stale day or two old ones, they were good donuts. I sat up and reached for the bag greedily! I snatched the unexpected present out of his hand and said, "Don't you know better than to bring donuts into a cop shop? Anybody sees these and they'll get confiscated!"

He laughed and said he had already left some in the front for the others. Maybe this kid was brighter than I was giving him credit for. Lordy, those donuts were fresh and smelled like heaven itself. I ate a couple and shared bits with Maggie while the kid got set up.

"Why you here so early? Skipping school." Of course, he wasn't. He said the kids had a day off for some sort of teacher training day. The kids didn't have to go in, but the teachers did. Nice, I thought. We'd have the whole day together. By the end of this day, he'd be begging me to tell him more.

"So, what happened," he demanded as soon as he was set up. I was still licking the sugar off my fingers. I took my sweet old time. Letting your audience stew a little is always good for a storyteller to do. I learned that listening to the old guys around the fire. By the time I finished hobbling over to the sink and washing my hands and drying them very carefully, that kid was about to jump out of his skin. I lurched back to the cot, sat down and said, "Now, where were we again?"

He gave me a blow by blow of what I had told him the day before. Danged if he hadn't been listening after all!! I settled into my cushy little throne and started up again.

"Waiting for the busy waitress, she told me her name was Darcy, not LouLou von Sugartown like Barney had introduced her. I smiled and told her a little about my life and who I was, just so she would get a feel for the kind of guy I am. I thought knowing me a bit would make her feel more like helping me. Nearing the bottom of my first cup of coffee and her first soda, she yawned really big. Didn't even try to hide her boredom. I decided the time to get her attention had arrived. I told her about the contest the town had announced. There was a what's-it-to-me attitude that just dripped off her face and saturated her whole body. She was about to call for the check when I said in a conspiratorial voice that there were only five people older than me and I needed her to help me get rid of them so I could win the prize.

"Her eyes flew open and she said indignantly, 'I'm not going to help you kill someone.' She started to slide out of the booth and said she was calling the cops. I grabbed her wrist and said, 'No killing and there's $50,000 for your efforts.' She slid back into the booth. She looked at me, askew. I looked her directly in the eye. The waitress came over and asked if everything was OK. Darcy said everything was fine, but we'd need menus after all. I told her just to order for herself because I was strapped for cash since I had spent all my dough getting over to see her act. I was grateful when she said she'd cleared enough tips to spring for breakfast. My empty belly gave a growl of happiness and we both smiled.

"We talked about little things while we waited for the food to arrive. Then we ate without talking. I was so hungry I didn't stop until I was done. But, when I was finished, I dabbed at the corners of my mouth with the napkins, real gentlemanly and all. Some manners I had been taught had stuck with me.

The kid chuckled and I looked up. He said, "I guess you'd be a vagabond gentleman then?" I thought about that for a moment. I kinda liked that. I nodded, puffed out my chest, pretended I had lapels on my shirt, tugged on them and continued my story.

"She ate more delicately that I did, so I politely waited for her to finish. I felt like I should apologize for eating so fast but then, did she really need to know I hadn't had real food for a long time? I decided not. When she laid down her napkin, she said, "Now tell me what is going on."

"I explained about the town's plan and how there were only six of us who were potential winners. Then I told her about SnotGun and how he got his nickname. I told her how rich he was and how he didn't need any of the things the town was offering for the prize since he already had more than the town did. Then I told her about his bad heart and how he was laid up in the bed at his house. I paused there. She nodded here and there and asked a couple little questions. When I was done, she held up her glass for a refill. I could tell she was thinking. She kinda had the same look in her eye Maggie got when she was mulling things over. I almost expected her to sneeze like Maggie did when she decided to help me out.

"She took a sip of the freshened soda and, over the lip of her glass, said, "So what would I have to do?"

"I had her! I knew It! This was going to be great. Even though, on the inside, I was skipping like a dog through a bacon factory, I kept my voice real calm and easy like and said that she'd need to take me home first. On the way, I'd explain the plan. If she was still interested then, she could come back that night and we'd do some spying and planning. She paid the check.

The kid interrupted me there. "So, she agreed?"

I said, "Oooooo yeah. We rode back here and I told her the whole plan. By the time we got here, I could tell she was getting into the idea, even adding bits of her own to make the plan better. I had her drop me off in front of the bakery so she wouldn't see my fine home and told her I'd meet her in this same spot after her show that night. The kid sat there typing and nodding like he was pleased with the whole idea. When he quit typing, I mentioned my throat was drier than a nun's fanny from the donuts and all the talking. He danged near dropped his laptop on the floor, getting up and half running down the hall to get me some more coffee. I was beginning to like this kid more and more.

He came back with the coffee and settled in.

"So, she came back in the middle of the night, right?" he asked.

"Nope."

The surprise on his face was priceless. Keep 'em guessing and keep 'em interested! I took a big drink of lukewarm coffee and grimaced. He'd forgotten to nuke the cup. I looked at that besotted face and didn't have the heart to send him out again. I told you I'm basically a nice guy, no matter what anyone else says. I set the cup aside and continued.

"After I'd slept a few hours, I decided to go back to the library for a bit more research. Maggie and I walked down the alley to the front of the bakery and who did we see sitting there in her car, big as day, but Darcy. She was staring off down the street like she was expecting something. I walked up and tapped on the window. She jumped but smiled when she saw me.

"I opened the door and asked if she liked dogs? She nodded so I stepped back and let

Maggie jump in. Darcy got all girly and grabbed Maggie's face, cooing to her like a baby and rubbing her head. I couldn't tell if Maggie was struggling to get away or wiggling hard from enjoying the attention. When Darcy stopped the rubbing to look at me, Maggie jumped up and licked her face, demanding more attention. I guess she approved.

"I asked her what she was doing there. Darcy said she was so excited about this plan that she'd gone back, gotten her stuff out of the hotel there, and left a note on the door of the bar telling Barney she'd quit and was all moved in at a motel at the edge of town. She added that she didn't think I'd want her to stay at my place. She had no idea how right that was!

"I told her I was just going to the library to do a little more research. She offered to drive me down there so we could talk more. She was quiet as we drove down the street. I noticed that she was looking around paying attention to everything. When we pulled up in front of the library, she said that her mother used to live here. She told me all kinds of stories about this place. Everything she described is still here, just like in the stories she told me. I nodded and said, "Things don't change much in this place."

"I wasn't in the mood to saunter down memory lane, so I got out and walked into the library. We spent all afternoon looking at the old yearbook and planning what to do. When we were done, she dropped me off at the bakery again. I got out and turned to thank her for the ride. She had a pensive look on her face and, without looking at me, said, "I don't think we should wait. Let's get this done. I'll be back around eight to pick you up here." I nodded, pleasantly surprised, and agreed.

CHAPTER

In the late evening just after dark, we drove up
the long tree-lined private lane and parked close
to the house, but not so close we'd be heard.
I already knew, because of SnotGun's allergies,
there would be no dogs around. We crouched
in the bushes and watched until the lights went
out on the bottom floor. In the upper right, only
one window glowed softly. I told Darcy that was
where we were going. Darcy was dressed in her
nurse's uniform and carrying those crazy high
heels. I made her put the purple curtain around

her in case anyone happened to look out at the wrong moment. That white dress did not make for good camouflage. She and I walked as quietly as we could around to the side door and slipped in. We shuffled up the dark stairway to the door to SnotGun's room. I cracked the door and made sure SnotGun was alone. He was still the same way I left him a week ago.

"I slipped over to his bed and whispered his name. His eyes opened and he smiled. "I thought you forgot about coming back," he said.

"Nope, I smiled, "And I brought you something to cheer you up." Both eyebrows lifted slightly.

"Can we tip your bed up a little? I want you to have a good view." He pressed the controls and arranged himself comfortably.

"Ready?" I pulled a small music player out of my pocket and put the speaker near his head. "May I please introduce to you, Miss LouLou Von Sugartown!"

"Right on cue, Darcy stepped into the room

and started walking really sexy-like to the foot of the bed. I looked at SnotGun, hoping he was impressed. He was definitely smiling and watching her. I glanced up at the monitor. None of the lines were jumping more than the others. Getting him excited enough might take a few minutes in his condition. She threw her stethoscope on the bed and tossed her hat at him. The hat slipped off the side of the bed. I started to go get the prop, but then decided I could get the hat later. Darcy started taking her clothes off, slowly piece by piece, leaning against the bed, hiding behind the curtains, showing off her skills. She dropped the dress in a puddle on the floor, stepped out and was just about to take off her bra when SnotGun raised a hand to stop her. She froze. He motioned her to come closer to him.

"She sidled up to him and leaned over. I heard him whisper, 'Darlin, I thank you for all you are doing, but I'm too sick to appreciate all that fine work.' He kissed her hand and said he was truly grateful what she tried to do for an old man. He told her to go to the chest of drawers across the room and bring him his wallet. I told him that wasn't needed, this was a gift to him for all the nice things he did for me. He told her to bring the wallet anyway. When she came back, he pulled all the money out and, without even counting the bills, handed them to her. Darcy took the money, thanked him and started gathering her clothes. SnotGun shook my hand and said, "I have to pay her because I know you don't have two nickels to rub together. You never have, Scabby." My jaw tightened. Under his hacking laugh, I heard Darcy gasp loudly.

"Darcy stood at the end of the bed and stared at us in total shock. Her jaw was hanging open. She was gasping for air and trying to say something. SnotGun asked if she was dying or something. I asked her what was wrong. She pulled her clothes up tight against her near naked chest and choked out the question, your name is Scabby? Oh my god, you are Scabby? I said I was. What did that matter?

She stammered when my mother told me about you. Who is your mother, I asked? Her name was Marcie and I was coming here to look for you. You are, oh my god, you are my father! She screamed out the last part. I fell against the chair behind me and ended up on the floor. She just stood there, staring at me with tears rolling down her face. I was too shocked to believe what I was hearing. Marcie had a kid. That kid was a stripper and that stripper who was standing right in front of me thought she was my daughter? This as too much. For a second, I was afraid I was about to join SnotGun on his death bed.

Then I heard an odd sound from SnotGun and picked myself up to see what was going on. SnotGun was grabbing his chest and his face was turning red. He began slapping his hand on the mattress and choking even harder. He took a while to get his breath and then I heard him say priceless! Only you Scabby! Only a loser like you!

That was when I realized he was laughing! I was furious that he was here to witness this. I hated him in that instant for laughing and her for telling me this in front of him. I was about to tell him off when all the bells and whistles of his machines started braying. The lines on the monitors were bouncing off the charts. Red lights blinked everywhere.

I didn't wait to find out what was going on. I grabbed Darcy and ran for the hidden door. I closed the door behind me just as the real nurse raced in. She was on a cell phone calling the ambulance. Darcy breathed raggedly as we stood in the dark. I could feel her eyes on me even though I couldn't see her. I said shut up. Do not say a word. We have to get out of here. I let her have enough time to pull the dress on and take off those crazy shoes.

We ran down the stairs, across the lawn to the car and drove back toward town. Every time she started to say something, I told her to shut up and drive. I broke the silence only to ask if she got all her stuff. She softly said I think so. I couldn't decide if I was angry or scared. If SnotGun survived, he'd tell everyone what I did. And worse he'd tell everyone the stripper was the daughter I never knew I had. I was not ready to let people know this little secret! If he died, well, I had helped him toward a better place and was one step closer to the goal. And he had gone out laughing ... at my expense. I figured he deserved the result for enjoying my discomfort so completely.

By the time we got back to the bakery, I had calmed down. She pulled over to the curb and heaved a huge sigh. I looked straight ahead. Finally, she blurted out that she was sorry. She was just so shocked when she heard my name. Her mom had never told her my last name, just called me Scabby. I wasn't sure what to say. I opened the car door and slipped out. I told her I needed a little time to get my head around this. She said can I come to your place? No, I told her, I need to be alone. I'll meet you at the diner at noon tomorrow. I left her.

I looked over at the kid who was staring at me with a stunned face. You had a child you didn't even know about? I looked up at the kid and pursed my lips up into a rueful smile. I guess I did. I gotta tell you, I continued, my legs were wobbly and my head was spinning as I walked to my box. I didn't even say hello to Maggie who was waiting patiently. I just fell asleep right away. I woke up feeling heavy in my chest. I wondered if I was feeling bad about the night before until I felt the heaviness move. Maggie lay on my chest instead of beside me. I scratched her ears and told her what had happened. When I finished, I felt like I understood enough to go talk to my ... I couldn't say the word ... not yet. I'd have to keep calling her Darcy for a while ... maybe forever."

I told the kid, "That's enough for today."

"No! He yelled, "you can't stop there."

I heard Pete call from the office, "Everything OK in there?"

I hollered back that we were fine and told the kid, "Look, this was hard for me to talk about. Go home, write up your notes and come back this afternoon." He reluctantly did as he was told.

Almost Brilliant

CHAPTER

When the kid showed up later that afternoon, I was ready. The morning's confession had taken a lot out of me, but a nap and time to regroup had settled everything again. He said nothing when he came in. Just went to his spot, got situated and looked at me.

"Let's get started," I said. He nodded, fingers poised over the keyboard. "The next morning, I went to meet Darcy. She was sitting in a booth at the back of the diner dressed like a nun. Not a real nun, just buttoned up from head to toe, neck to knees. No makeup or jewelry. I was surprised. I sat down across from her and waited. She stared at the table and wouldn't look at me, but said she knew most people met their father when they were pretty much naked but not when they were 43 years old. That made me laugh out loud. I bent down a bit so I could see her eyes.

"'Look,' I told her, 'I gave this a lot of thought this morning and I decided that we need to talk about this today and then just move on. After last night, we never need to see each other again until I get the money and give you what I promised.'

"She looked at me from under her real eyelashes. Without all the make-up, she almost looked like a much younger, less harsh woman. Then she asked, 'Is that what you want?'

"I didn't know how to answer. 'I guess so,' I said. 'I mean, I never meant to make a relationship out of our arrangement. We were supposed to just be two donkeys on the same mountain path going in opposite directions, just squeezing by each other, as we moved on.' She smiled at my choice of words.

"'Well,' she said, 'that's where we differ. My mother loved you. At her age, I was a surprise for sure. She knew how you felt about kids and families from things you'd said over the time you were together. She left here while you were gone because she knew she was pregnant, and she knew you wouldn't want to get married or anything. By the way, in case you are wondering, she never married or even spent much time with anyone else. You were the love of her life.'

"I thought about those words and what I had missed out on. That surely explained her mother's crying and odd behavior that week before I went out on that week-long job. Darcy lifted her head higher. 'When mom died, I decided to come here to find my father and see if we could, at least, become friends. That's part of why I came to this place with you. When you said you knew everybody. I figured I'd get you to help me ... you know, find, well, you!'

"I shook my head to try to make all the thoughts fall into place. She must've thought I meant I didn't want to know her because she started to leave again. 'Fine, if that's the way you feel. I'm gone.'

"I put my hands up to stop her. 'No,' I said, 'Sit down. You're going to have to give me time on this! I've never had a family. Being an orphan, I don't even know what family life is like. Other than Maggie and the brief times I've had roommates or lived with your mom, I've always been alone.'

"After a bit of time, Darcy reached across the table, put her hand on mine and said, 'If you can make room for Maggie, maybe you can make room for me too.' I gotta admit that brought a tear to my eye."

I thought I heard a sound from behind the typewriter so I looked up to see how the kid was doing. He was just dropping his hand from his face and beginning to type again. He sniffed a little and looked up with chagrin on his face.

"Gotcha, huh?" I asked. I smiled at him and he smiled back. I continued with the story.

"Darcy and I talked for a couple more hours. Then I took her on a tour of the town, showing her all of the places her mom had talked about and I even showed her the house we had lived in together. At dusk, we had dinner together and talked more. That was a surprisingly good day. She asked if she could see my place.

"I said, 'Not tonight.' I wasn't ready to become a dad and let the daughter I'd never even envisioned see me as a failure all in the same day. We agreed to meet the next day for breakfast. I went back to my box and slept fitfully all night, dreaming of her mother and what might have been.

"When I got to the diner the next morning, she was dressed in her everyday normal again, make-up and everything. She looked happy. The coffee I ordered for me and soda for her was on the way to the table. When I sat down, she pushed the newspaper across the table at me and said, 'Next?'

I let my brows knit as if I had no idea what she was talking about. She tapped the headline – Local millionaire banker dead of heart failure. I felt all the wind leave my lungs. Suddenly my eyes refused to focus, and I felt faint. When I could see, I read the headline again. My breath came back heavily. She reached out and took my hand, and said, 'Easy. Breathe. Breathe."

"When I felt steadier, I read the article. The report said that Creed Remington had been found by his nurse in his bed last Saturday night in the throes of a heart attack. Attempts to revive him hadn't worked. He was pronounced dead on arrival at the hospital. Darcy looked at me with a smile when I glanced up. 'I didn't really think my idea would work,' I said. Shaking my head sadly, I told her, 'I didn't really want to kill him, you know. Just incapacitate him enough to be out of the running.'

"'Well, planned or not...' She paused and

looked around. When she was sure no one was looking, she pulled her tank top down a little to show off the top of her breasts, shook them slightly and said, '... he definitely went with a smile on his face.' Even I had to laugh at that."

The kid was smiling too when I looked over. "So, you really did kill him," he asked.

I made a face and said, "Kinda and kinda not. My plan to excite him into a near fatal heart attack by sending him a stripper hadn't killed him." He had, after all, told her to stop before the good parts. (I felt a little dirty talking about the woman I now knew as my daughter that way.) "So, what I did didn't kill him. But his uproarious joy when he heard who Darcy was and then rejoicing so rigorously in my discomfort ... that was what killed him. Everything was his own fault," I said. "If he hadn't been such a prick and had had some compassion in that creaky old body, he wouldn't have laughed so hard and wouldn't have done himself in." I leaned forward.

"So, you see, Kid, I'm not guilty of killing SnotGun no matter what you may hear. He did that all by himself, the mean-spirited old coot." I could tell the kid was not impressed. "I'm not going to try to convince you now," I continued. "You just remember this. I'll tell you the rest of the story and then, at the end, you can decide. For now, you go home and get rested up. I want to think about how to tell you the next part."

"When you tried to kill another one, right?" he whispered.

"No, Kid, aren't you listening? I didn't kill anybody. I just helped things along a little!"

CHAPTER

"Let me introduce myself please. I'm Virginia Ann Jenkins, R.N. That's right, I'm a nurse and have been for over twenty years. I'm not given to flights of fancy. I don't play silly games nor try to become a friend to my patients. I'm here to do a job and I'm very good at caring for people. Some of the situations I've worked in were odd. Different. Strange things often happen when you deal with critically ill patients and their families. But there's something truly odd going on in this town ... and I'm determined to get to the bottom of what is happening.

"I came to work for Mr. Creed Remington who'd recently had his second massive heart attack. The prognosis wasn't good. With no family on which to depend, I was therefore needed on a 24/7 basis. Since he was willing to pay the rate, I gladly took the position and moved into one of the many guest rooms in the house. I took care of him for a week and he seemed to be recovering, interacting a little more every day. Each day his vitals were a bit stronger and he was beginning to show more interest in food and the outside world. He had even asked to have the television moved into his room.

"I'm still stunned that he died the way he did. After checking on him and making sure he was doing well, I'd gone to bed. I'm a creature of habit and my bedtime is ten, but I sleep lightly and have a monitor set up in my room down the hall in case of emergencies. Around midnight, I woke up feeling like something was wrong. Music was coming from the monitor beside my bed, but I could barely make the sound out.

"When my curiosity finally drove me from my bed, I considered getting properly dressed but decided I just would pull on my robe and check on Mr. Remington. When I was in the hall outside the sick room door, I thought I heard laughter, loud, roaring laughter. I stopped at the door and listened, thinking that he was watching a television show. I was pleased to hear him laughing so delightfully. I started to go back to my room. I was halfway up the stairs when I heard the alarms go off. I raced back to the room and reached for the doorknob. I leaned on the heavy door and pushed it open.

"There on the bed, Mr. Remington was clutching his chest. His face was florid, and his lips were turning blue. The screaming monitors showed a failing heartbeat. I pulled my phone out of my pocket and called 911. Then I climbed onto the bed and began CPR. I was sure I had lost him well before the ambulance arrived, but I did not give up. I never give up. That's just not my style.

"When the EMTs burst through the door, I climbed down, stepped aside and watched them do their work. They quit trying to revive him after about five minutes and pronounced him dead. I stepped over to the monitor and looked at the EKG print out. The lines were normal for a long time and then suddenly became erratic. I knew I needed to show the strip to his doctor. The strip suggested that something had come out of nowhere and frightened or upset Mr. Remington.

"I began to straighten up the room. That was when I found the truly odd thing. Under the end of the bed was a nurse's hat. The cloth was crisp and clean, but the style of the hat was not the one I preferred. There were initials on the inside ... not mine. Like I said, 'Something odd is going on here."

CHAPTER

12

Trying to decide how to tell the kid about Faith Chandler took me some time. The next day when he showed up, I decided I would start from the beginning ... which, of course, was grade school. He came in and set up his equipment. Then, without being asked, he took Maggie for a trip outside. I didn't tell him that I had taught her to pee in the floor drain by the sink and she didn't really need taking out anymore, but why stop him from doing something Maggie enjoyed so much? She deserved to get out once in a while even if I couldn't take her.

When he got back, I launched right in. "So, today we talk about Faith Chandler."

"Wait," he said, "what about your daughter? What happened to her?"

"Patience, kid! You'll learn all about everything in due time!"

I launched into the next part of the story. "Sweet little Faith was in my classes all through school as well. She didn't have a nasty nickname. She was the sweetest, kindest girl in the school. Even though she was quiet, she seemed to sparkle with joy every day. No one disliked her or made fun of her in any way. Not only because she was nice to everyone but also because her dad owned the only local bakery. If she called him, he would send pastries over to us any time of day. He loved her so much and there was nothing he wouldn't do to make her happy. I had great memories of sitting behind her in my desk and leaning forward to whisper, 'I think we need some donuts' when we were supposed to be reading. She always got up and walked to the teacher's desk. And the smiling plump teacher always let her go use the phone.

"When Faith finished high school, she decided that, having worked in her dad's bakery all her life, she wanted to be a pastry chef. I heard she went to some prestigious cooking school in France intending to spend a year there. But she was back home within six months. Being in that huge city had been too much for her gentle small-town soul. She left a happy young lady, sparklingly full of life. When she arrived back in town, she was sad, drawn, and pale from sheer homesickness. Her once-lustrous hair hung like limp cords of dull black yarn. Everyone bemoaned the loss of the joyous little girl and hoped she'd return some day.

"A few days after her return, she went to work in her parents' bakery again, but instead of doing the everyday cookies, cupcakes and other bakery staples, she started doing specialty cakes and other magnificent desserts she'd learned in France. Eventually, she got so busy that her father bought the shop next door and helped her turn the little space into her own cake shop with a big picture window and work-tables just inside in a big U shape. Anyone walking by could actually watch her putting the final touches on cakes right there in the window. People from other towns even came by to see what she created. There were cakes of every kind – from little kid's birthday cakes with animals and trains to five and six-tiered wedding cakes full of flowers and leaves. They were true works of art.

The kid stopped me, "So that's what the boarded-up window next to the bakery used to be?" I nodded.

"When her dad and mom passed away, Faith just moved back into the old space. She missed them so much that she quit making fancy cakes and just did the regular stuff. She told people she was just too sad to make beautiful things anymore.

"Was she ever married," the kid asked? I shook my head.

"Not that I know," I said. "I never heard of her dating or anything. She just loved her cakes. In fact, she loved them too much. She had to sell the bakery a few years ago because she couldn't quit eating her work. She gained a lot of weight and got diabetes. The last I heard she was in an assisted-living place where they made sure she could only eat what was made for her and no sugar was allowed. She had lost a lot of the weight, but she was never the sweet, happy person she was ever again."

"So, that's where she was when you ..."

I knew he was about to say something I wouldn't like. "Don't say it, Kid! Don't you dare! I did not kill her! Just like SnotGun – this was not my fault! That was a pure D accident of nature!"

The kid shook his head silently and returned to his keyboard. I think he's beginning to get me. "So, your daughter stayed here," he asked. I tipped my head and calmed myself with a deep breath and even smiled a little bit.

"Yes, she did for a while. I have to admit, after a bit, when I realized she wasn't going to start calling me 'daddy' and all that stuff, I got to liking having her around." I decided not to tell him that Darcy had since gone to stay with friends in the city for a while till all this blows over. No sense getting her involved in the scuzzy wig. And no sense giving him head's up on the favor I was going to have to ask him later.

Anyway, I drew myself up on the pillow throne and got comfy again, and said, "Tell me where we are." I watched him as he recapped the last time we were together. Maybe, since he was coming to visit and sticking to this project, I ought to stop calling him kid. I smiled to myself.

"Ok, Frankie, let's get on with this." I saw his head snap up out of the corner of my eye. Bingo! Effect achieved! I ignored him and kept talking.

The smile on his face as he typed was genuinely happy. He pulled himself up straighter and typed with intent.

"When I saw Faith again after she came home from France, she looked awful. Her hair was limp. Her skin was blotchy. She walked with a beaten-down hunch to her shoulders. She didn't look much like the pretty girl I'd gone to school with at all. I saw her again several months after she had opened her shop. The change was magnificent. She was smiling and happy again. Standing upright and proud, except for the times she was bent over one of her creations. The more people praised her, the more confident and beautiful she became. I always got a kick out of the fact that she always seemed to have a dot or two of frosting somewhere on her face. She looked so cute. Soon, the fact that she was taste-testing her goods a lot became all too noticeable.

"At first, rumors flew around town that she'd come back from France pregnant. But when the allotted time came and went, everyone had to acknowledge that she was expanding in more than just her creative culinary skills. Over the years, we all watched her go from a petite little girl to a rotund bouncing woman. I say, bouncing because her workspace didn't expand as her girth did. She often turned and bumped into a table or a cart and seemed to bounce back. I sat on the bench out front one day and felt like I was watching a little yellow ducky in a circus shooting gallery. Turn, bounce, ping, all day.

I heard Frankie smother a chuckle. I could almost hear the fat jokes percolating in his head. I shook my finger at him. "Don't you think I'm being disrespectful," I demanded. "There will be no fat jokes here. Not about her. She was still a lovely person. I'm just telling you the facts so you understand the reason everything happened."

Frankie nodded and wiped the smile off his face. "You know," he said, "Pardon the pun, but I think you might've been a little sweet on her yourself."

I smiled and nodded, "Yup, me and every guy in town. I never even tried because I knew I didn't stand a chance." I heaved a sigh. "I realized many years ago that all the guys in town must have felt that way because very few had the nerve to approach her over-protective parents to ask if they could date her."

"Fast forward to five years ago," I changed the subject. "She had to sell the bakery, mostly because she was too heavy to walk any longer. The bakery wasn't wheelchair accessible and the business was no longer good enough to pay for expansion. I was there the day she handed over the keys. I almost wished I was a photographer on that day. The terrible sadness on her face as she gave the new owners the keys and the delight beaming from their faces was as they dreamed of their future was so moving. She sat in her wheelchair for nearly an hour in front of the building before the aide she'd hired to help her insisted they move on. I heard she moved into that assisted-living place because she had nowhere else to go." Frankie nodded and asked, "Her parents were gone and no siblings, right?" I just nodded. "So, she just languished away there?"

I shook my head. "Rumors flew around as they always did in a small town. The aides that worked with her were glad to sit in the diner and swap stories about her even though they knew they shouldn't."

"They talked about how, for a long time, she refused to even get out of bed. When she was forced to, she just stared out the window. She refused to eat and got so sick they had to put her in the hospital. She was diagnosed with diabetes, kidney failure and came pretty close to dying.

"Then one day, like a light had been relit inside her, she just sat up and said, 'Enough!' and started getting better. No one knew why, but she started eating right and went to the gym and rehab every day. The weight started coming off and she began to look like herself again. The diabetes had taken its toll though. She had some kidney and liver damage and her eyesight had dimmed significantly enough that she decided to stay in the complex after she had found a new home.

Frankie asked, "She was number two on the list of people between you and the prize, right?" I nodded and, as much as I liked her, I had to find a way to get her out of the way. Notice that I didn't say kill her. But I knew she had enough money to live out her life in this place so she didn't need the prize. Maybe she'd go back to Italy. I heard she had people there. I just needed her out of the picture."

"That's when Maggie and Darcy started in on you", Frankie encouraged. He actually winked at me, but I ignored that little jibe. I pursed my lips and continued with my story. I hadn't told Darcy about my living conditions yet. "I usually met her at that dingy hotel she stayed at or at the diner and we talked. Every time she brought up the idea of visiting my place, I ducked the topic.

"One night, I was lying in my box with Maggie beside me, stroking her ears. I could tell by her snoring she was asleep. I must have dozed off a bit too. I dreamed that I was running after someone. When I woke up, Maggie's little legs were flailing all over. She muffed a couple times in her sleep. I watched her dreaming and wondered, for some reason, what Faith dreamed about. I decided the time had come for me to go visit her.

"The next morning, I met Darcy in the park with my bag of stale doughnuts. Darcy asked if I had decided who our next target was. I sort of whispered Faith's name and Darcy nodded at me. 'She's next. Any idea how we can take her off the list?' she asked.

"I wiped my hands and explained Faith's condition. I didn't have an idea yet. But I remembered the look on her face when she created those cakes, how happy she was. I told Darcy that Faith had to be missing something in her life to take the place of all that baking. As far as I knew she had no other hobbies except walking every day.

"Darcy's eyes lit up. 'We can follow her on her walks and push her down a cliff.' Laughing, I shook my head and told her to look around. The closest thing to a cliff in this place was the curb in front of the hardware store that was higher than most. Darcy drew her lips into a mini grimace and nodded.

"'Wait a minute,' Darcy said. She started digging through that suitcase she called a purse and pulled out a bunch of papers. She sorted through them until she waved one at me. 'Her birthday is next week.' I shook my head and said, 'So?'

"'So, I think we need to help her celebrate.'

"'Tell me more.' The more Darcy talked the more I liked the idea.

"'We could make a huge cake and slip up to her apartment to share her day with her.' I said that sounded good but I didn't know how we'd get in to visit her.

Darcy figured the whole thing out quickly. She said, 'I'll call her and pretend to be a fan. I can make up a story about how her cakes had been the best part of all her birthdays when I was young, and how I just heard about all Faith's troubles. And then, I'll wangle us an invitation to lunch.' She bobbled eyebrows on her forehead like a couple of caterpillars doing the fandango. I laughed.

"'And,' I coaxed... 'And?'

"Darcy shook her head and continued, 'We get her to eat the cake, her blood sugar goes crazy, she goes in to a diabetic coma and voila!"

"I sat back. 'But only into a coma, right?'

"'Definitely,' she whispered.

"'That could work, I said, as long as she doesn't die.'

"Darcy said firmly. 'Of course, we'll be very careful!'

"I leaned back and nodded for a few minutes

thinking the plan over. Then I thought of a couple of problems I asked her, 'Darcy, can you cook?' She just smiled at me. 'Where are you going to make this cake?'

"She looked down and said, 'Let's go for a ride.' We got into her car and drove a few blocks. A few minutes later, we pulled up in front of a very familiar house – the one her mother and I'd lived in together. I sat there staring, letting dusty, bittersweet memories flow over me.

"I stammered, 'Wha, wha, what are we doing here?' Darcy pulled her keys out of the ignition and jangled them at me. She got out, walked up onto the porch and unlocked the door. She stepped inside and beckoned me to follow.

"I reluctantly got out of the car and shuffled my way up the walk. Maggie followed Darcy without hesitation. Big as you please, she just wandered in the door and started exploring the rooms I stopped at the door. 'What are we doing here?' I asked again.

"Darcy threw her arms out and said, 'I decided, if we were going to do this long-term project, I wasn't staying in that ratty hotel any longer. I rented this place and I got a job in town. I'm now a real resident of this little town.' She stood there smiling at me. I honestly didn't know what to say. The place had many changes – paint, wallpaper, carpets – but the house was still the place I'd lived in so long ago. I started to tell her I didn't want to be here, but when I saw the pride in her face, I didn't have the heart. Hell, what was the worst that could happen? Maybe she'd let me shower once in a while.

"She continued, 'We need money to pull this off. You can hang out in the diner. I can meet you for lunch. That place is a hotbed of conversation and gossip. After a day or so, no one would pay attention to you sitting there drinking coffee. Everybody goes in there and talks about everyone else. More importantly, they listen to conversations that they aren't part of, hear things they shouldn't and pass that information on too. They just can't wait to repeat anything.'

"She said, Just sit in the back booth was away from the tables where the gossips liked to sit. Everything we need to complete our tasks will be pretty much available there.'

"I thought about the sense of that idea and had to agree. I'd heard more things in that diner than I ever wanted to know over the years. The whisperings about old Miss Kearney, the town's supposed witch, dancing "sky clad" (what she called naked) in the moonlight in her back yard on full moon nights was too much for my little mind. Some things need to be kept to one's self.

"I looked at Maggie, who was now lying on the floor nearby like she was waiting to find out what we were going to do next. Her eyes shifting between us as we talked. When she saw me look at her, she lifted her head and then sat up. After looking at Darcy and then at me once more, she sneezed her 'let's-do-it' sneeze. Darcy gasped.

'I thought you were kidding,' she said. 'Maggie really does get what you're talking about, doesn't she?' I nodded.

Frankie stopped typing. I looked at him. "So, you just started planning a party for Faith?"

I said, "That was the plan." I hung my head and added, "And that's how Darcy found out her father was a bum."

I made Frankie go home on that sad note, refusing to say another word. I needed a few hours to think out how to tell him the rest of the problem.

CHAPTER

Frankie didn't come in the next day. I lay on my bunk scratching Maggie's ears and thinking. Two days later, he showed up, looking tired and worn out. I looked at him like I was disappointed in him. But before I could say anything, he apologized and said that he'd taken mid-term exams over the past two days. Because he'd been working on this project so much, he hadn't had enough time to study. He thought he did ok and he was ready to get back on this project now. I decided not to chastise him. In fact, I felt a little bad about keeping him so busy.

"So," he said, "tell me what happened next." I told him that I was going to fill him in on the plan Darcy had come up with and also that had Maggie's approval. He nodded. I continued my tale with the fact that I met Darcy at her house the following day.

"'While I was there, Darcy phoned Faith and told her the elaborate story we'd concocted. I sat in amazement, listening to her make up the story on the spot complete with incredibly intricate details. I couldn't hear the other end of the conversation, but I could hear the sound of a happy voice coming from the phone.

"Darcy fabricated a fantastic tale about her eighth birthday and a beautiful pink cake Faith had made just for her. She stopped talking, listened for a few seconds and then said, 'Right, the cake had rainbows and unicorns all over the top.' I was stunned. Faith couldn't possibly remember all the cakes she'd ever made and Darcy had never even seen. But Faith seemed to be buying the story Darcy was selling and intending to pay full price.

"Darcy kept smiling and looking over at me, nodding and smiling. I continued to listen, while Darcy went through a couple more "cakes" she had supposedly enjoyed on other birthdays. About halfway through the conversation, Darcy let slip that she loved decorating cakes too, though she'd never be on Faith's skill level. Darcy's smile broadened as she listened to the excited voice on the other end of the line.

"After happily chattering for almost half an hour, Darcy let her voice change while she talked about how she had heard how sick Faith had been and told her how bad she felt for Faith's troubles. Again, she was silent for long minutes, letting Faith talk. She added a few 'hmmm's' and 'ohhhh's' here and there.

"When Faith started to wind down, Darcy said she didn't want to presume anything, but she was enjoying this conversation so much she didn't want the pleasure to end. There was a long pause, and then Darcy's eyes lit up. She gave me the 'thumbs-up' signal. A second or two later, she said into the phone that she'd love to come and visit. Maybe see pictures of other cakes Faith had made. There was another silence for a few seconds and Darcy said, 'Really? Your birthday? Why I'd love to come visit on that day. No one should be alone on their birthday!' She made a few more arrangements and then said good-bye. She turned to me, dusted her palms together, and said, 'Dam I'm good!' I almost hugged her.

"We sat down at the table and figured out exactly what we were going to do. We put together a grocery list and she said that she was going to see Faith in two days. She'd have to get the cake made today and put the icing on tomorrow. I asked if she needed my help and, much to my relief, she said not with the baking. But, if I could find a pretty box down at the SuperStore big enough for a two-tiered cake, that would be the best way to help. I said I would, although I knew I didn't have any money. Maggie and I would just have to find enough cans and bottles to cash in.

"I let Darcy drive me back to town and drop me off before going to get the ingredients for her present. Maggie and I would have to spend the next day dumpster-diving while she was baking. Bright and early the next morning, I got my stuff together and off we went to find enough redeemable bottles or cans.

I sat up and stretched a bit. "You doing ok, Frankie?" He nodded and looked up. "You look tired," I said.

"I am," he yawned, "But this story is worth being a bit tired for. Keep going. What happened next?"

I told him that I found about ten dollars' worth of bottles. 'I hated that buying a lousy box was going to cost me so much beer money but, in a long run, this would be a small price to pay ... I hoped. By mid-day, I didn't think I had found enough redeemable items to have enough money, so I decided to go to my best 'fall back' plan. I decided to walk over to the blood bank and donate. I had known the folks there for years and they knew my situation. They also knew I only came to them as a last resort when I really needed money. I suspected they paid for my donation out of their own pockets. I should have felt bad, but I just didn't. Ten bucks is ten bucks. That's not much money for a person with a job, but it sure meant a lot to me.

"I was coming out of the lab, counting the money, when I heard my name. I turned and saw Darcy standing down the street in front of the drug store. 'Scabby? What are you doing here?'"

"I smiled and said, 'Just giving the gift of life.' She looked a bit confused until I pointed to the sign in the window of the building I had just come out of. Then she smiled and said, 'Maybe I should do that while I'm here as well.'

"For some reason, I didn't want her to go in

so soon after I'd been in there. I distracted her by asking what she was doing here. She told me she had come into town for special decorations for the cake but couldn't find what she needed at the grocery store. Someone told her there was a specialty section in the drug store that might have what she needed and, she patted the bag on her arm, they did.

"'Are you going home?', she asked.

"I said, 'No, I was going to go buy the box.'

"She said, 'Come on, I'll give you a ride.' Then she could take the box home with her. We drove over and she told me about the cake she was making. She'd decided chocolate on chocolate would be the best kind of cake to make. What sugar-holic could resist chocolate? I agreed. I barely had enough cash for the box and ribbon – which I never would have thought of.

"When we got back to town, she asked if I lived above one of the stores by the bakery. 'They look like they might have apartments above them,' she commented, gazing up at the second story above the shops. I made a non-committal sound and changed the subject. I told her to drop me off at the bakery. I said I wanted to see if I could get a peek inside Faith's old bakery so I could help her add details to her – I air quoted – 'memories'. Darcy smiled, dropped me off and then pulled away. I pretended to look in the window until I heard her drive around the corner. Then I went to my box in the alley.

"Maggie was waiting for me. I knelt down and rubbed her ears. She searched my pockets to see if I'd brought her anything. I felt terrible that I hadn't thought of her. We walked over to the dumpster and I climbed up on to an old wooden box that I kept there for when I needed a step. I leaned into the smelly enclosure to see if there was anything for Maggie inside.

"I almost fell in when I heard someone scream my name. I felt someone grab my ankles and almost broke my legs pulling me back. I fell backward and crashed on a soft pile which gave a soft 'oof' sound. I looked under me and there was Darcy. I slid off her and yelled, 'Are you trying to kill me? What are you doing here?' She said she was tired of me evading her questions about where I lived so she followed me. I was furious with her.

"'Now you know what I didn't want you to know,' I screamed at her. 'I'm homeless. That big box Maggie is peeking out of is where I live. I didn't want you to know about this. I wanted you to think better of me.'

"Darcy sat there with tears in her eyes and looked at me. 'Don't you feel sorry for me, dammit,' I yelled. 'I lived my life just the way I wanted to and never thought I'd live this long. I chose not to accept everyone else's idea of responsibility and I never regretted that choice until recently.' I flapped my hand at her and told her just to go and let me get some sleep. She looked like she wanted to say something else. I got up and, with as much dignity as I could muster, I brushed off the seat of my pants. Then I crawled into my home and pulled the flaps in around me. I heard her walking away and wondered what tomorrow would bring."

Frankie sniffed a bit and kept typing. I yelled at him, "Don't you start! Do we need to stop for today?" He shook his head and stared at the keyboard. "Danged soft-hearted fools," I muttered.

About that time, Pete came down the hall with my dinner. I told Frankie to go home and get some rest. The next day was time enough to finish this story. He didn't want to leave, but finally agreed. The kid was tired and so was I.

CHAPTER

The next day he showed up with donuts again. I figured the day must be Saturday since he was there early – it's easy to lose time in jail. Every day is just the same. Without commenting on the previous day's story or giving him the chance to comment, I picked up telling him my tale.

"I was just about to walk to Darcy's place the next day when I saw her sitting in her car at the end of the alley. I got in. Neither of us said anything about the day before. I asked her to take me to the gas station. When she asked why.

I told her that I could clean up there and she said no. There was no reason why we couldn't go back to her place and get me a shower if I wanted to clean up. I didn't disagree.

"When we got inside, she said she'd make us lunch. 'And, by the way,' she said, 'I was planning to surprise you later but check the second door on the right.' I walked down the hall and looked into the room she pointed out. There on the bed were clean pants, a shirt and even underwear. I picked them up and examined them like they were an alien product. I hadn't worn underwear for years. I took them to the bathroom, took a long hot shower and tried to remember how to put the underwear on. I whispered to myself, 'The opening goes in the front, Scabby.' I smiled at my dry wit and razor-sharp humor. Speaking of razors, Darcy had thought of everything. On the sink were a razor and shaving cream, a comb and even a new toothbrush. I cleaned up and looked in the mirror. Though I lamented my lack of a haircut, a guy I hadn't seen for a while looked out. Older than I remembered but still familiar.

"I went to the kitchen. She looked up and smiled. 'You look good,' she said. I indicated the clothes and said, 'You did good. Thank you.' She waved me off and pointed at the sandwich on the table. 'Eat while I box the cake.' I watched her lift a beautiful cake up and put the delicate dessert into the box. The chocolate frosting looked to be at least an inch thick. I'm not much of a chocolate eater but I would have liked even a piece of that. 'The cake looks great,' I said. 'Well, from what I've heard and the pictures I saw,' Darcy said, 'the result was nothing like what she could do. I'm just hoping it's been so long since she had chocolate that she'll give into temptation.'

"We loaded the cake in the car. She asked if I had ever been to the assisted-living facility and if I knew anything about the layout of the building. I laughed and said, 'No, the likes of me in my normal condition wouldn't be welcome there.' She muttered that she hoped there was no security in the front lobby. I told her if there was, I would create a scene that would let her get by with the cake and then I'd sneak up soon.

"She pulled into a parking spot in front of the three story, columned, brick building. The lawns were manicured. There wasn't a leaf out of place or an extra bit of dirt anywhere except where soil belonged. I told Darcy that I doubted birds were even allowed to fly over this place. Darcy whistled under her breath and whispered that she was glad we'd cleaned up."

Frankie interrupted, "Are you talking about that big brick place by the park?" I nodded. "Huh," he said, "I always thought that was some kind of hospital."

I said that it kinda was. Faith had gotten so comfortable there that she simply stayed on. She'd nowhere else to go unless she wanted to move back to Italy with her parents' family. Her parents' insurance and the sale of the bakery left her fairly well off. She would be able to live out her days there." I looked him right in the eye. "See," I said, "another person who didn't need that prize." Frankie nodded and, without comment, poised his hands to start up again.

"Fortunately, although there was a security desk, no one was in the lobby. We walked in calmly and glanced around as we crossed the carpet to the elevators. According to the directions Faith had given Darcy, we had to go to the top floor corner apartment. We rode up the elevator in silence. When the doors opened, we stepped out and looked at the numbers on the wall ahead of us. An arrow with the apartment number we wanted pointed to the right. We looked down the hall and saw Faith's room at the end. The deep pile carpet muffled our steps as we passed a few other doors and stood in front of the one we wanted for a moment. Then, almost as if we'd planned the action, both of us took a deep breath and blew air out. I raised my hand to knock just as the door flew open.

"Faith stood in front of me, hardly recognizable from the last time I'd seen her. She had the same jet-black pile of hair that made her 5-foot frame a full two inches taller – though even I could tell the color had come from a bottle. She wore no makeup or jewelry. Despite her now stick-thin figure, she wore a giant billowy Hawaiian-print house dress in brilliant reds and yellows so bright they made my eyes hurt. She took Darcy's hand and shook it heartily. Then she turned to me. She squinted at me, then frowned and said, 'You'll have to forgive me, as my eyesight has dimmed a bit but I know you, yes?' I swallowed hard and, judging from her greeting of Darcy, mentally prepared myself for a happy-attack. I said, 'Yes, Faith. I'm Scabby. Remember me?'

"Her squeals of delight probably disturbed the dead. She threw her arms around my neck and rocked us back and forth. I had trouble keeping my balance. When she leaned back, she said, 'Thank you, thank you so much for thinking of me and coming to visit. I remember you from school. You were always so nice, even when that mean old John Talley used to pick on me. I remember you punched him once for me. I'm so glad you're here.' She squeezed me up close to her. When she relaxed a little, I slipped out of her reach and she invited us in. I didn't correct her by telling her I'd punched John Talley because I'd just caught him as he stole a Twinkie out of my desk. I was happy to let her think I was her hero.

"We stepped through the foyer into a beautiful sunlit room. Darcy set the beribboned box on a side table near the door. In front of the window, Faith had set a table for two. She gasped and scampered into the kitchen, apologizing over and over. She hadn't been prepared for two visitors, but setting out another plate would only take a few minutes. Darcy and I looked around the room while Faith happily chattered away, setting another place. 'Finally,' she said, gesturing like a gracious hostess would, 'There now. Please come in and sit down.'

"Judging by the way the room was decorated, Faith seemed obsessed with white. The walls were flat white with a few bright splashes of color where pictures hung. The table set for three now was made of metal painted white. We pulled up the tiny white wire chairs that matched the table. I wasn't sure the one I had would hold me, let alone anyone else. The white tablecloth glistened in the diffused natural light. Even the dinnerware was white, but a thin strip of gold ran around the edge with an elegant capital "C" in the middle. Faith had artfully designed plates full of cut vegetables – crudité, she called them – and tiny sandwiches made of cucumber and cream cheese that were only big enough for one or two bites. In the center of the table stood a clear pitcher of a yellow liquid I assumed was lemonade. 'I hope you don't mind eating a bit healthy today,' she said. Both of us smiled, assured her the food looked wonderful and passed our plates so she could play gracious hostess. After she'd passed around the rabbit food, she filled our glasses and said the lemonade was sugar free, but she might be able to find a little sugar if we needed some. Darcy took a sip. She grimaced but said the flavor was perfect. I left my glass alone.

"We ate the little sandwiches and veggies while the two women chattered about cakes. I put in a detail here and there, but mostly I just listened. When we'd finished and the table had been cleared, Darcy said, 'We brought you a small gift.' Faith's hands flew to her reddened cheeks and tears welled up in her eyes. She gasped and said that was all too much. Guests and a gift. This would be the best birthday she'd had in a long time.

I looked over at Frankie. "I gotta tell you, Kid. I was starting to feel a bit guilty over what we'd planned. I mean, she was just so happy about everything."

Frankie nodded and said, "But I bet you did go through with the plan anyway, right?"

"Well, yes," I said. "Darcy was leading the way. I had no choice! I had to just sit there and watch what happened."

"Darcy brought the bright pink box with an enormous multicolored bow on top over to the table. 'I brought you something I'm pretty sure you haven't had for years, Miss Faith.' She stood up and walked to the side table where the box sat waiting. When she returned to the table, she placed the box gently down in front of Faith. Trembling hands ran over the top and sides of the box, delicately touching the bow and ribbons. I heard a slight sniff come from Faith. Darcy walked back to her chair, sat down and told Faith to go ahead and open her gift. Faith's hands shook as she pushed the ribbon aside. 'This looks so delicate and lovely,' she simpered. Her squinting eyes were feverishly bright with joy as she opened the top and peeked in.

"The instant she saw what was inside, she flew up out of her chair so quickly that the fragile seat clattered loudly against the floor tiles. The table jerked and dishes rattled as she pushed herself away. She ended up standing against the wall with her arms outspread like a convict caught in the act. Her eyes were full of terror. If I hadn't known better, I would have thought there were poisonous snakes inside that box.

"Darcy rushed to her side and touched her shoulder gently. Faith began gasping and muttering, 'Take it way, take it away, it's beautiful, I love it, I can't have that here, take it away...' over and over. Darcy patted her shoulder and shushed her until she calmed down. I reached over and set her chair upright.

"After a couple long minutes, Faith finally caught her breath and looked at Darcy and then at me. She began apologizing for her actions. She hadn't even seen chocolate for years ... even the smell had taken her by surprise. With all her troubles, she hadn't allowed herself to even be near any sugary treats. Darcy guided her back to her chair and said not to worry. She was sorry. She just thought that since this was Faith's birthday and Faith had made so many wonderful cakes for her, she just wanted to do something small to return the favor. Faith said she felt bad for reacting so strongly. She looked at the cake, then stood up and went into the kitchen. She returned with two plates, two forks and a big knife. She perched herself on her tiny chair and said, 'This is ridiculous. There is no reason that you two cannot have a piece. I'll just sit and enjoy the company while you two enjoy the cake.'

"She cut a large piece and handed the plate to Darcy, who then in turn, passed the delicate China to me. When I took the plate, she held on tightly for a minute. I looked at her and she glowered at me and very gently shook her head back and forth as if telling me not to eat the cake. I figured she was upset because the plan had had a little hiccup. But I couldn't see why she was mad at me. Faith refusing to eat her cake wasn't my fault. But that cake looked and smelled delicious and I was going to have some.

"I tried to tug the plate out of her hands. She held on, white knuckled. She puckered her face up into a tighter angry grimace and less subtly shook her head from side to side again. She looked madder than a boxful of badgers as she finally let the plate go. I gave her my strongest 'get-over-it' look and plunked the plate down in front of me.

"With one last warning glare at me, Darcy looked back at Faith and said, 'Please not such a big one for me. I have to be on my feet all day, so I need to be careful of my weight.' Faith said she totally understood that and then went off on the story about how she'd let her weight get out of control and how hard she'd had to work to get her figure back again. She said she wouldn't wish that battle on anyone.

"While they were talking, I took a big forkful of that luscious cake and lifted the wonderful morsel toward my mouth. Out of the corner of my eye, I saw Darcy vigorously shaking her head at me. I thought, 'If she didn't want me to eat the dessert, she shouldn't have made the cake look so good.' I defiantly shoved the whole fork into my mouth and smiled. The frosting melted in my mouth, coating my tongue with sweet joy. Darcy sighed and took her plate from Faith. I noticed that she picked at the cake part and moved the bits and pieces around, but she never even tasted a bite.

"I glanced at Faith. She was staring at the cake as if mesmerized. Darcy put a small amount of cake and frosting on her fork and leaned over to Faith, like a mother teasing a reluctant child to try a new food. With the cake inches from Faith's quivering lips, Darcy urged her to try just a little taste. 'One piece of cake won't make you overweight again,' she said as she patted Faith's hand. 'You can live a little on your birthday and then get right back on healthy tomorrow. You've been good for so long and one little taste of the cake I worked so hard to make just for you won't hurt.'

"Faith flicked her tongue out like a cat stealing cream and licked the bit off the fork. Her eyes closed and pure joy covered her face. She opened her eyes a second later and stared at the cake. As if in a catatonic state, only her head moved back and forth very slightly, Faith watched Darcy pick up the knife and cut another piece of cake. She put the plate down in front of Faith's huge awe-struck eyes and put a fork in her hand. Like a robot, Faith cautiously dipped her fork into a small piece and then lifted the chocolate to her lips. She paused, looked at us, and then, ever so slowly, she slipped a delicate bite into her mouth. Darcy followed her every move, mimicking her mouth opening and lips wrapping around the fork. As Faith eyes closed again in sheer ecstasy, Darcy leaned back and sighed.

"Faith opened her eyes and proclaimed that the cake was a slice of heaven. She loaded her fork again, this time with a much bigger piece, and said she'd forgotten how amazing chocolate tasted. 'Diabetes be damned,' she said, and tore into the cake like a starving prisoner of war.

"When the plate was empty, she reached into the middle of the table and pulled the box to her. I was stunned to see her start tearing the cake apart with her hands, shoveling fistfuls into her mouth at a time, barely taking the time to chew and swallow. Chocolate flew everywhere. I'd seen nature videos of lions tearing apart antelope that were less violent. I looked over at Darcy, who was sitting back in her chair with a full-moon smile on her face.

"Then, as suddenly as she'd started, Faith stopped. Her face was covered from nose to chin and ear to ear with chocolate. Her hands were dripping with the guts of the cake. She screamed and jumped up again. 'Oh my God what have

I done!' She knocked the box off the table and began shaking her hands. Chocolate flew in every direction, decorating the pristine walls in glorious splotches. The sterile clean floor was suddenly splattered with brown globs.

"Faith looked at both of us and screamed, 'Get out! Get out of here! Now!' Instead of the blissful creature she had been a few minutes ago, she now looked like the alien that jumped out of that guy's chest in that movie. She sure as the devil scared me! I got up and began sidling towards the door, but Darcy stayed where she was and tried to calm Faith down. She couldn't get close enough to the screaming woman who kept flinging her hands in every direction and chanting, 'Get out! Get out!'

"Then, without warning, Faith took off running towards the kitchen sink in a blind panic. As she turned the edge of the counter that divided the dining area from the kitchen, I saw her foot hit the upside-down box that had held the cake.

Then everything began to happen in slow motion.

"Her foot hit the box. The box slid over the frosting that had been stuck to the top. Faith's legs went out from underneath her and flew up, flopping around. Her arms flailed in the air, as her body seemed to float for a few seconds. Both Darcy and I reached forward in a futile attempt to catch her, but we were too far away. We heard a sickening crash and saw her bounce a bit as her head caught the sharp corner of the counter. She crashed to the cold floor, flat on her back and didn't move. Neither did Darcy nor me.

For a few minutes, we stood motionless. Then Darcy burst into action. She picked up the plates and spoons we'd used and shoved them into that suitcase of a purse she carried. She took everything off the table that showed that anyone else had been there. Then she turned to me and hissed, 'Let's get out of here.'

"Faith lay motionless. I asked, 'Is she dead?' Darcy pulled a mirror out of her purse and put the glass under Faith's nose. There was no indication of breath. 'Oh, crap!' I said. 'Indeed,' said Darcy and added, 'that wasn't supposed to happen. Come on!' she urged, pulling me towards the door.

"As we passed the phone, Darcy stopped and called 911. Because she panicked, she did a convincing job calling in an accident. When the dispatcher asked her name, she left the phone lying on the table. Then she grabbed my arm and we went to the door. She opened the door carefully in case someone had heard all the commotion and was coming to investigate. No one was in the hall. On the way to the elevator, we passed a stairway. Darcy stopped me, pushed the door open, and jerked me through that opening. We went down the stairs, her half-carrying me and came out on the side of the building. Calmly as we could, we walked to the car, got in, and drove off."

I heard Frankie let a breath go. He must have been holding his breath for a while. "Oh, man." He said, "This time you did kill her."

"No, I didn't!" I yelled at him. "She fell. The result was an accident. Just like what Darcy said – that wasn't supposed to happen. I had nothing to do with the accident," I wailed, so angry I was shaking inside. Frankie shook his head and started typing again.

I forced myself to calm down and then continued my story. "Anyway, we didn't talk on the way back. When we pulled into Darcy's driveway, I got out and started to walk back toward the road. She asked where I was going. I told her I needed to go home. She said she was pretty sure I needed to stay at her house that night. I turned and looked at her defiantly. I'll go get Maggie but you need to stay here. You'll know why in a few minutes.'

"I was about to refuse more adamantly when the first cramp hit me and bent me in half like a folding lawn chair. Darcy said, 'Yup, you're going to need to be here. Come on.' She helped me into the house and into the bathroom.

"I was in there for a good forty minutes while everything I'd ever eaten in my life came out of my body. I hurt so much from the cramps that raced through me I could hardly sit up. Fortunately, there was a handicapped rail by the toilet. I held on to that metal rod like a lover I hadn't seen in years and moaned until things slowed down. I heard Darcy tap on the door. She asked, 'Are you OK?' All I could manage was a weak groan. She took that to mean I was still alive. She said she had some tea in the kitchen when I was ready. My stomach turned over at the very idea, but I held on.

"A few minutes later, I cleaned myself up as well as I could and stumbled out to the kitchen. I was so weak that I had to lean on the wall. By the time I made the short walk to the table, I was exhausted enough to go to bed for a month. Darcy set the tea in front of me and sat down on the chair across the table. 'I tried to tell you not to eat that cake,' she said. I stopped with the cup halfway to my lips and looked at her. I put the cup down and said, 'What did you do?'

"She looked down at her cup and said, 'Remember the other day when you saw me coming out of the drug store?' I nodded. 'Well,' she said, 'I wasn't in there for cake decorations. I bought two boxes of Ex-lax.' My eyebrows shot up and my mouth dropped open. 'That's right,' she continued. 'You know. Ex-lax, the kind of laxative that looks and tastes like chocolate. I melted the medicine into the frosting.'

"Once again, I was stunned. 'Why on Earth would you do that?' I roared as loud as I could find the strength to yell. Darcy shrugged and put her hands out, palms up. 'I was just trying to hedge our bets. I figured, if the sugar didn't make her sick enough, then she would get diarrhea so bad that she'd get dehydrated and her kidneys, which were already bad, would give out. I didn't tell you because I needed you to act normal and I didn't think you could.'

"I couldn't believe she was so ruthless. She leaned over and looked at me sadly and said, 'Stop thinking I'm the bad one. It wouldn't have hurt her much.' She sat back and continued, 'Besides thinking about what happened, we didn't actually hurt her. She let her fear do herself in. And we actually made her last few minutes on earth very happy ... just like we did the other one." I just looked at her and shook my head. At least she had decency to be sad about the accident.

"Then another wave of cramps hit my so hard my head started spinning. I told Darcy she was going to have to help me, as Nature seemed determined to keep pressing my poop button even though there was nothing there. She groaned at my poor attempt at humor.

"I must have passed out because the next thing I knew I was in the emergency room. They kept me overnight to get the diarrhea under control. I think Darcy stayed all night. I know I spent a lot of time looking up at someone dressed in white that I hoped was her.'

Frankie had stopped typing somewhere in the story. He was shaking his head too. "You did it," he said. "You killed her."

"No," I told him, "Darcy was right. She did herself in and we made her happier than she'd been for a long time before she died." Frankie picked up his materials and left for the day without another word. I sure hoped I hadn't lost him. I needed him to believe me so I could get the real story out.

CHAPTER

15

Frankie came back the next day. He seemed angry. Instead of shuffling down the hall and into his spot, he strode into the cell and stopped at the door. He stood, arms akimbo, and stared at me. For several minutes, I stared back. Then I let out a long drawn out, "Yeeeeeeessssss?"

He said, "Tell me that you honestly believe that you did not kill any of the people they think you killed. Tell me this all works out in the end. Tell me I'm not typing a pack of lies just to help you get out of jail."

I took a moment and then slung my plaster-encased leg over the edge of the bed and stood up. I brushed the imaginary wrinkles out of my pants and shirt. Then I stood up tall as I could, put my hand over my heart, looked him square in the big owlish eyes and said, "Why would I lie to you."

That took a little steam out of him. He walked halfway to his place and turned around. "So, if I go talk to this Darcy," he said, "She will confirm everything you told me?"

I said, "When I said, when she gets back, I'm sure she will."

His eyes narrowed, and he half-turned his head, all the while keeping eye contact with me. I'd never seen him so assertive. Maybe I was a good influence on him.

"Gets back?" he repeated, and his voice only cracked a little bit.

"Yes, she got called back to the city for something to do with a sick friend. She should be back as soon as she feels like she can leave them."

He looked for a moment like he was going to bolt.

I said, "Kid. Frank. We have gotten so far. You gotta trust me. I need your help." I reached out and touched his arm. "No one else can help me."

He heaved a huge sigh and stage-whispered, "Fine." Then he turned to set his area up.

I settled back into my little nest of pillows and waited until he was ready. "So? You're good with everything so far? You understand what happened and everything? No questions?"

He said he was good and that we should get on with the work.

CHAPTER

16

"As a responsible health care provider, I felt obligated to report anything suspicious that I found in regard to any of my patients. Since Mr. Remington had no relatives with whom to discuss my thoughts, I decided to visit the local sheriff and remind him of my discovery. I took the hat I'd found under the bed to the jailhouse and confronted the obnoxious man about my concerns. He pointedly told me to get a grip on my imagination. He'd lived there all his life and knew everyone. There was no one in this town who'd kill Mr. Remington. After a few minutes, I left graciously, but not happily.

"After I left Mr. Remington's employ, I was hired to be one of the in-house nurses at a local assisted-living home. The institution was an upscale place with occupants who were largely mobile. The only thing they needed was a person to answer minor medical questions or send them on to a doctor. My duties largely consisted of tending to minor scrapes and bruises and acting as a sort of companion to the loneliest of the residents.

"A few days after I had started my new job, there was a curious incident that made me wonder just what had happened. I felt a bit bad about what happened because I had been called away from my desk overseeing the front lobby to assist an elderly man who'd fallen. About 15 minutes after I returned to the desk, I was surprised to see the police show up with all lights flashing and sirens blaring. They told me about the emergency. We raced up to the room from where the call had originated.

"Inside was a mess. There was chocolate everywhere. I knew something was wrong immediately. I told the EMTs that this was wrong. Miss Faith never ate chocolate. She was diabetic, had fought her way back from morbid obesity and was rabid about never eating sugar again.

"As I was explaining myself, I turned to see the irritating sheriff enter the room. I'd never actually seen a grown man roll his eyes before. That simple act infuriated me, but I held on to my emotions with an iron will and painfully clenched jaws. I told the cops to look around carefully. I told them this wasn't right. But the sheriff contradicted me.

"I walked over to him and told him I had suspicions. He crossed his arms over his chest and said, 'What now? Did you find an extra pair of socks in the wrong drawer?'

"I gave him my most evil do-not-mess-with-me look. He did not back down and neither did

I. I told him why I thought this was odd. To his credit, he listened, but he didn't take any notes.

"After the EMTs took the body out, he left me to deal with the mess and said he'd check out my concerns. I called the janitorial service. While I waited, I looked the table over. I brushed a crumb off one of the wire chairs so I could sit and wait. Some of the chocolate was on my finger when I looked down. I couldn't resist the temptation and took a quick lick before rising to wash my hands. The flavor was amazingly good, but there was an odd under-taste that I couldn't quite place. I decided to put some in a zip lock bag and keep what might become evidence. I'm not sure why I did, but I kept the bag in my pocket until I got home.

"I'm telling you something was going on."

CHAPTER

Maggie greeted Frankie with a wild wag of her tail when he arrived next. She never barked and didn't do the usual dog stuff – jumping up and licking – but, when she wagged her tail at someone, I knew she was glad to see him. Sure enough, he murmured hello to me, gathered up her leash and took Maggie out for a stroll. Our Maggie was no fickle female. If you fed her or walked her, you were her friend.

When they returned, I said, "Ok, I want to tell you about Beefy McGuire next."

"Beefy?" he said quizzically.

"Yeah, his nickname is a good story. His real name is Keith. We played basketball together for years from fifth grade until I quit school and even then, we played pick-up games on the weekends in the parks. I know I don't look much like a b-baller, but I was. We made a great team. Beefy was tall, lanky and had huge hands that could hold a basketball in either one easily. He could land a basket from almost anywhere on the floor. He also was the best free-throw shooter we ever had. But he wasn't good at defense. I, on the other hand, was little enough and fast enough to dodge in and out of those big galoots, steal the ball and feed the ball to Beefy for the scores. No one could guard me because I was so quick. The three other guys we played with were happy to shoot when they got the opportunity. After I stopped going to school, they continued to play together until Beefy stopped, too. They were a good team, but never as good after I left. And they weren't even a team anymore when he quit. "

"So how did he get his nickname?" Frankie asked.

"I was just getting there," I said. "You need to know about Beefy's little sister. He was twelve when she was born, and that kid loved Beefy from day one. When she was learning to talk, she couldn't get her lips around his given name which was Keith. She could only manage to lisp 'Beefy'.

"His whole family started calling him Beefy which embarrassed him to death. He made everyone promise not to call him that in public and we respected his wishes; his family did because they loved him, and I did because he threatened to beat me to death with my own arm. Beefy was really kind and easy going for the most part, but I saw him mad once when someone picked on a little kid. I was truly afraid of the angry Beefy from that day on and I decided I never wanted to get on his bad side.

"Anyway, the team won enough games to get to the finals the first year they were on varsity squad. I watched every game from the stands and made sure Beefy knew I was there rooting him on. They were in tenth grade and as proud of themselves as peacocks in full feather. On that last day of the tournament, they were up against their archrivals from over the river. They played neck and neck down to the last few minutes. All ten players were drenched in sweat, they played so hard. During each break, people would go out onto the hardwood with dry mops to run over the floor and make sure it was dry.

"Our team was down two points with five seconds left when they stole the ball and Beefy was driving to the basket. He was ready to lift of for a beautiful layup when a rival knocked into him so hard, he fell flat on his back. The ref awarded him two free throws. Our crowd went wild. The other fans groaned. Everyone knew about his 80% free throw record. One of the guys helped him up off the floor and asked if he was ok. Beefy grimaced and then smiled. I sent him mental messages, 'All you need is two, tie the score up and you'll win in overtime.' I liked to think he heard me because he looked up at me and nodded as if to say, 'Piece of cake.' One of his teammates patted him on the butt as he jogged by and they went to their places along the lane.

I looked over at Frankie. "You play any ball?" I asked. He nodded and said he wasn't very good. Academics were his strong point, not sports. I said, "But you have gone to games and cheered for your team, right?" He nodded. I said, "So you understand what is at stake here."

He said, "Sure, if he makes both shots, you tie the game and go to overtime. If he misses, the game is over." I nodded and said, "Not only that, rumor was that there were college scouts in the stands. A win could get Beefy to college in the only way he had a chance."

"Beefy stood at the line and bounced the

ball. The arena was nearly perfectly silent, both sides holding their collective breaths. He took his time and launched the first shot. Perfect! The ball dropped through and barely disturbed the net. The place erupted. One more to tie. A teammate retrieved the ball and handed it back to the ref next to Beefy. From the stands, I gave him a thumbs up and crossed my fingers. The room went quiet again. Beefy bounced the ball and took aim. Just as he was about to shoot, his little sister screamed out, "You can do it, Beefy!"

"I saw his face blanch at the sound of the nickname. He lowered the ball and frowned as he heard a wave of giggling began to drift through the arena. Then the audience started chanting, "You can do it Beefy! Go Beefy Go!" He was embarrassed and unnerved. Then he lined the ball up to shoot, but he tipped slightly sideways as the ball left his hand. The ball flew wide. The audience gasped."

I stopped telling my story, thinking about the

look in Beefy's face and the sound of his sister calling out. Frankie asked, "What happened next?"

"We lost. Beefy was so embarrassed about that hated name that he never went on the court again. In fact, he quit school the next day. No one could talk him into going back. He let that little problem ruin his life.

"He moved out of his parent's house and we got a place together. Of course, his parents blamed me and said I was a bad influence pulling him away from the church and his family. I didn't care. I had my friend back with me.

"We took jobs whenever we could find them and spent all weekend drinking our money away. I should have felt bad and I should have made him stay in school, but I already knew I'd never go to college. I was just so happy to have my best friend with me that I never gave his family's anger a second thought. Poor Beefy never escaped that hated nickname, but he learned to deal with it.

"After that day, we played together at the local YMCA where there was an adult basketball program open to anyone. Our first year, we played against every rival we could find and beat them all. We were small-town heroes. Everyone wanted to be our friend. We went to parties every weekend. That's where Beefy learned to drink under my excellent guidance. And we drank copious amounts every weekend. Beefy's parents were super religious so, at first, he had to sober up enough to be ready for church every Sunday. After a while, as long as he was at church and had dinner with them once in a while, they pretty much let him be on his own. Of course, nobody gave a crap where I was or what I was doing.

"We lived happily for about ten years, until Beefy collapsed at a party one weekend when he was in his mid-20s. Someone called an ambulance to get him to the hospital. I clambered into the ambulance, claiming kinship. As soon as we got to the emergency room, I was pushed out of the way. I watched through the windows in an alcoholic stupor as they worked on my friend. When they closed the curtains, I sat down on the sofa in the waiting room. I must have passed out. I woke up because someone was shaking me. I looked up and saw a very blurry security guard. He told me I had to leave. That I couldn't sleep my night of partying off there. Explaining why I had to stay took a while, but I finally made him understand I was there for my friend. The nurses confirmed that I'd came in with one of the patients. The guard nodded and let me stay at the desk. The nurse said Beefy was very lucky. He'd nearly died. As I was standing there hanging onto the counter so I wouldn't fall, his parents came through the door.

"The second his mother saw me, she flew into a rage like a mad little tigress. She started beating on me, calling me every name in the book and blaming me for her baby being there. I stood and took the blows because I knew she was right. Beefy's dad pulled her off of me and nodded toward the door. I left and didn't talk to Beefy again."

I looked over at Frankie. He was staring off into space with the saddest look in his eyes. "What's up, Kid?" I asked. Frankie sniffed softly and Maggie's ears perked up. She knew that sound.

Maggie uncurled herself from her place at my side and went to Frankie. She sat down directly in front of him and stared up. He shook his head, took a swipe at his eyes and replied, "I had a best friend like that once."

I said, "Once?"

He nodded, "He was my brother. He died a couple years ago."

I said, "I'm so sorry for your loss."

Frankie sat up and proudly said, "He was a soldier and a hero." Then he sagged a bit, scratched Maggie's ears and continued, "But I still miss him."

I nodded and said, "How about we call it a night?"

Frankie smiled weakly and gathered up his things.

CHAPTER

When Frankie came in the next afternoon, he apologized for his emotions. I told him not to worry about anything that happened in our visits. I added that I was sure now that he understood how important my friendship with Beefy was and how lost I felt without him. To find his name on the list of people that were between me and the prize was the most upsetting of all. I wanted Frankie to know that Beefy was the last person I'd ever deliberately hurt.

I settled into my place. Maggie jumped up and

curled in to her place by my side. Frankie settled in and said, "Ok, I'm ready."

"Well, like I said, I hadn't seen Beefy for years. I'd heard through the grapevine that he'd gone back to the church, married a woman named Bitsy who was a miniature version of his mother and settled down. He went back to the church, became a minister, and he and his wife had three kids. He seemed to have a great life in spite of wasting his youth in decadence with me. But I never saw him, even though I sometimes walked past their house after a late-night drinking with the boys.

I paused for a minute – for effect and all. When I knew I had Frankie's attention, I continued. "Well, except for that one time when he threw me so far under the bus, I nearly never got up again. There were questions all over Frankie's face. I waved a hand and said, "Let's get to that part of the story."

"One night," I continued, "when I was hanging out at the river with my drinking buddies, someone started telling stories about Beefy and his wife. Seems as though, after his kids grew up and left the nest, the wife sort of lost her mind. Like his mother, she'd always been very religious, but having to split her attention between the kids and the church had kept her pretty balanced. However, each of the children, when they left the house, had also left the church. The wife was furious about this and she hounded the kids until they finally told her some version of how much they hated being the minister's kid and how her heavy-handed demands for them to be extra good because of their position had made their lives miserable. Each child left town for a new life at the earliest opportunity. Just before his last daughter left, his mother, now a widow, moved in with them, and they turned their zeal totally on the only other person in earshot."

I shook my head, feeling sorry for Beefy all over again. "Having experienced his mother's full-on wrath one time, I can only imagine what his life had become with two such harpies running everything."

Frankie asked, "Are you talking about physical abuse here?"

I shrugged. "Like I told you earlier, Beefy was a sensitive guy. He never liked to hurt anyone or see anyone get hurt. His mother had completely ruled his life except on the basketball courts and those few years I took him out from under her thumb. I am sure, if the wife was as much like the mother as I was told she was, when they started in on Beefy, he just went along with whatever they wanted in order to keep the peace.

"Anyway, the guy said Beefy was drinking again. I scoffed, but the guy said he knew someone who was buying booze by the case and making a delivery to him once a month. That explained why I never saw him in the bars but, from then on, I kept my eye out for him. I would have loved to meet up with him and be drinking buddies again! I even had fantasies about how we'd laugh whole nights away again like we used to.

"On my fiftieth birthday, I'd been out celebrating with the guys. I was stumbling home after two in the morning and decided to walk past Beefy's house. I was happily stunned when I saw Beefy walking along the sidewalk on the other side of the street, all stealthy, staying in the shadows and carrying a big box. The night was so quiet I could clearly hear tinkling of glass bottles. Beefy was carrying a case of booze. The drunk's story was true. There was no way I wasn't going to see what he was up to!

"I followed him past his dark house and down the street. He turned into the alley. I went up to the corner real sneaky-like and peeked around the bushes. He was standing in front of an old shed a few feet down the dirt lane, unlocking a padlock. He pulled the lock off and opened the door. When he picked up the box and stepped inside, I quickstepped down to peek in. Just as I started to look in the dingy window, Beefy came back out.

"Since neither of us were fighters, we both screamed like a pair of little girls. Beefy's big old mitt grabbed the back of my head and he put his hand other over my mouth. He was shushing me and telling me to be quiet, looking around to see if anyone had heard us. I'd have gladly been quiet, but his hand was so big he was covering both my mouth and my nose. I was flailing my arms and pulling at his hand, not trying to get away, but just to keep breathing! When he finally looked at me, Beefy realized what was wrong and let me go. I fell to my knees, gasping harshly to get enough air into my lungs. He shushed me again and whispered questions at me. Why was I here? How did I find out? Who else knew? Did anyone see me?

"When I could breathe comfortably again, I put my finger to my lips and pointed to the shed. We slipped inside and pulled the door closed behind us. Beefy lit a small lantern, dimmed the wick way down and put the metal base on the floor. He looked at me for a long minute. Then with a huge smile, he called me a sorry washed-up whelp like he always had. I called him a couple of more colorful names and then we threw our arms around each other. We laughed and probably even cried a bit. We sat down on an old pair of tarp-covered lumps and started talking, like we'd never been apart. I'd missed this guy so much.

"After we'd talked a bit, I asked him what he was doing here. He explained that this old shed backed up to his property. His wife hated the rickety old thing because she thought the shed was an eyesore. When she said she wanted a privacy fence between the house and the alley, he'd built a tall one across the back of the yard and told her he'd pull the shed down when he had time. The fence was tall enough that you couldn't see the shed from the house. His wife forgot about the thing she hated. Well, then life got in the way. One spring, he'd planted the climbing roses and ivy his wife loved so much along the fence. They grew so thick that they covered both the fence and the shed. Since that time, Beefy had used the place as an escape from the overabundance of zealous hormones in his home. He ended his story by saying that an ounce of prevention – he jerked his thumb over his shoulder toward the fence –was worth a pound of manure – he tipped his head toward his house. I laughed and said I understood.

I asked him what was in the box he'd been carrying. He got a sort of 'deer in the headlights' look in his eyes and said that if he told me, I'd have to swear not to tell anyone. I, of course, agreed. He reached under a tarp near him and pulled out a bottle of gin. He looked at the clear liquid sloshing in the bottle and said, "Not my favorite, but this has no odor that could be detected by suspicious noses!" He nodded in the direction of his house. "Those two can smell alcohol like those fancy pigs in France can smell truffles!"

I laughed at the mental image I got of two pigs in dresses wearing going-to-church hats nosing through the mud and leaves. He opened the bottle and said that we had time for a drink or two for old time sake, but then he had to get back to the house. He took a swig and handed me the gin. I didn't care much for gin either, but beggars cannot be choosers as they say. He continued his tale.

"Whenever he was low on supplies, he had a friend who he'd helped in the past. That guy went to another town, bought a case of gin and brought the contraband back for him. Not wanting to risk being seen, Beefy went for a walk when the guy called him and met him a couple of blocks away from the house. I smiled and asked how he got out. He lifted the bottle in a salute. He said that his mother and wife were so busy in the evenings with their committees and outreach that they were used to him going for nightly walks to clear his mind. His youngest daughter still lived with them and she got roped into help every night. He could tell how much she hated it and talked about how sad he was going to be when she left him alone with them.

"I took a pull of alcohol and handed the bottle back. 'They're creatures of habit,' he sighed before taking another drink. 'Dinner at six. Paperwork or meetings from 7:30 to 9 and bed by 9:30.' He said he usually planned his walks for about 8:30 so they'd be in bed when he got back. They never asked what time he got back in. As long as he was in bed when they woke up, no questions were asked. Then he said, as much as he was enjoying this, he had to get back. I asked if I could join him again. He agreed but he reminded me that I couldn't tell anyone, and I was going to have to chip in for my share. I might even have to pick up the delivery once in a while. I thought picking up a delivery was a small price to pay to be reunited even for a little while.

"We stepped outside. Beefy locked up the shed and showed me where he hung the key on the side of the building. He said that if I got there before him any night, I should be sure to keep the door closed. We gave each other another awkward hug and said good night. I went down the alley in one direction and Beefy went the other.

When I got home that night, I crawled into my box and thought about how happy I was to have reconnected with my old pal. I fell asleep with a smile on my face that night.

Frankie looked up with a big grin. I could tell he understood how happy that meeting made me. He asked if I wanted him to take Maggie out for another short walk. I said agreed just so I could sit and savor the memories a bit longer.

CHAPTER

19

When he came back, the first thing Frankie wanted to know was how long Beefy and I kept meeting. I told him we met two or three times a week for a couple months. "Everything was going great. I'd taken over pick-ups because no one even blinked at seeing me walking around late at night pushing my shopping cart full of junk. Another box on top wouldn't alert anyone. Beefy was grateful. He'd been so worried about what would happen if his congregation found out he was drinking again or, worse, if his mother and wife found out. He said, 'They all think I'm a good, clean, wholesome man of God and I am. Well, except for this one little thing.' He tipped the bottle in his hand up and drained the bottle. 'Me too,' I added. We both laughed at that.

But all good things must end. One even, we were sitting in the shed sharing basketball memories. We hadn't even opened a bottle yet when we heard sirens. Blue lights flashed through the dirty newspapers covering the window and the cracks in the walls. We looked at each other like a pair of mice waiting for the eagle to land. The door flew open and police poured into the little room. They were screaming for us to get on the ground. I dropped but Beefy stayed upright.

He told them who he was and how he'd found me squatting in the shed. He fed them a malarkey story about counseling a poor soul to stop drinking and trying to help him give himself up to the Lord. He kept talking and telling the police a pack of lies that made him look like a hero and me like a bum. He told them that I'd broken into the shed a few weeks ago and he'd been meeting with me since then. He kicked an empty bottle over to one of the cops and told him that I'd tried to make him start drinking again but he'd remained strong. I lay on the ground and listened to the best friend I ever had tell lies and say that everything here was mine. He said he'd nothing to do with anything that had gone on in the shed before he found me. I knew the stories would be all over town by noon. The fact is that most lies usually travel halfway around the world before the truth gets the chance to pull its pants on!

Frankie looked up at me and shook his head. "How could he do that to you?"

I told him, "I knew Beefy was scared of his reputation being ruined but I didn't know he was a lying weasel."

"I guess you can't trust anyone," Frankie said as he turned back to his typing.

"I was sent to the jail. The sheriff and deputies acted like they had no idea who I was. I kept telling them that they knew me, that they knew I wouldn't do such a thing. They left me sitting in the cell with the door locked overnight. The next day my court-appointed public defendant came in and I told him what had happened. He said he'd look into things. There was no physical evidence against me, so I was likely to get off with a minimum sentence. He left after about 20 minutes. I was still sitting on the edge of the bed with my head in my hands when I heard Beefy's voice. I felt like jumping up and reaching through the bars, but the look on his face was so sad that I just stared at him.

"'Scabby, buddy,' he started, 'you have to understand I did what I had to do.' I didn't move or even blink. He kept talking, 'if I hadn't told them you'd been squatting in there, my mother and my wife would've been humiliated. The congregation would've lost faith in me and asked me to resign. Without the church, those two women would've never let me have a moment's peace. They would've ridden me to my grave. But you, Scabby, you'll come out fine. No one cares if you drink or steal or anything. You'll be fine.' He reached his hand through the bars like he wanted to shake my hand. 'I'm sorry,' he said. 'Please say you'll forgive me.' I looked him in the eye and said, 'Never.' I turned away from him and laid down on my cot and faced the wall. I tried not to cry as the best friend I'd ever had shuffled down the hall and out of my life.

"That is the saddest thing I ever heard," Frankie whispered.

I nodded and said "I think that's enough for now."

CHAPTER

20

The next time I saw Frankie, I told him how Beefy had died. "Darcy and I were talking about the next person on the list. I gave her the list with two names crossed off and three left to go. She chose Beefy. We were having lunch at the house. Maggie kept moving between us begging for scraps. Both of us kept slipping her little morsels of our ham sandwiches which kept here happy.

"I told Darcy my history with Beefy and how I had come to understand what he did but that I'd never really forgive him. Darcy said she could understand that. I told her that the elder Mrs. McGuire had died, and his wife, Bitsy, had taken over her duties as the matriarch of the church. She was part of a group of widowed women who seemed to be together all the time. They met for coffee daily at Beefy's house and went shopping and did their church work together. Rarely were any of them seen without at least one of the others. Even when Beefy retired from the pulpit, his wife was still active in the church. The women continued to flock together at his house.

"Darcy shuddered slightly and said she had seen them fluttering down the street, cackling like hens and clearing everyone off the streets ahead of them. In fact, she'd nicknamed them The Hens. I agreed that that was a good name for them and smiled at the image. She asked what we were going to do about Beefy.

"I had no idea. Like I'd said all along, I'm not a bad person. Even as much as Beefy's betrayal had hurt me, I never wanted to destroy him. In fact,

I figured that wife of his was punishment enough for one life. Darcy chuckled in agreement. She said she'd done some checking around. When Beefy left the church, they'd moved into a small house in the same area. His wife and her cronies were there every day except for their Wednesday church night. Beefy usually stayed home. No one visited Beefy. He had no male friends at all.

"Darcy thought we should go visit him some Wednesday night and strike up our friendship again. At first, I was strongly opposed but the more she talked, the more I could see the justice in her plan. Finally, I looked down at Maggie who was still there waiting for another handout. I asked, 'What do you think Maggie?' She stared at me and then turned to Darcy and then turned back. Me. Darcy. Me Darcy. Finally, she sneezed her approval. Both of us laughed, threw her a snack and began planning.

A week later, we went to Beefy's house and sat in the car a few doors up until The Hens left through the front door for the night. We could hear them cackling like a bunch of broody hens as they walked the two blocks to the church. When the echoes of their chortling had dimmed, I picked up the dark canvas bag I'd brought with me and we walked through the dark carport to the side door. I knocked and stepped back a bit. I heard clomping steps in the kitchen and Beefy called that he was coming. A few seconds later, he opened the door.

I was stunned to see him. He'd always been thin, but now he was downright scrawny. His hair was completely gray, and his face was drawn. Leaning heavily on a carved cane, he looked old and shriveled. His sunken eyes lit up and filled with tears when he saw me. For a moment, I saw the young man who had been my oldest truest friend. I offered my hand and said, 'Hello."

"Instead of taking my hand, he just stood and stared. Then he cried out, 'Well, butter my butt and call me a biscuit!" as he dropped the cane and enveloped my hand in both of his. In one practiced motion, he pulled me into a suffocating bear hug. I could feel every rib in his chest pressing up against me. He wasn't as strong as he used to be, but I could still feel the breath being pressed out of my lungs.

"He let me go and turned his attention to Darcy. I was so moved by his appearance that I almost changed the plan but Darcy, as usual, kept us moving forward. I introduced her as a friend, and he invited us in.

"We went inside, passing through a dingy kitchen to the attached dining room. As we went by, I dropped the bag I carried on the floor out of the way by the sink. I looked around and made sure I sat where Beefy would have to sit facing me with his back to the kitchen. Beefy had some coffee brewing on the sideboard in the dining room. He poured us each a cup. When he came back, I rubbed my hands over the scarred top of the table and asked if that was the same table that had been in his house so long ago. He smiled and said yes, that his wife and mother were very, uhm, frugal. He smiled half-heartedly and lifted his cup. We sat quietly sipping for a few moments.

"He asked how I'd been, and I decided to tell him who Darcy was. He was at least as surprised as I had been to find out I had fathered a child. But years of hearing confessions from his parishioners had schooled his face to remain steady. He stood up and hugged Darcy again. He told her how happy he was that his old friend wasn't alone. She smiled back and settled down to continue making small talk. We chatted for a couple of hours about everything under the sun, including how the church had left him in good shape. Because of the service of his family over the years, they provided everything he needed as long as he was alive.

"So," Frankie interrupted, "he had no need for the prize either." I nodded and said that made me more interested in going ahead. I returned to the story.

"We knew that The Hens were due back by 9 PM. At 8:30, Darcy excused herself to go to the restroom. Beefy told her to use the guest bath that was off the kitchen since that one was closer. While she was gone, Beefy took the opportunity to tell me how much he missed me and to apologize again for the way he'd treated me. He said that he'd tried to come see me again, but his wife had put a stop to his evening walks. 'She said she no longer believed the stories I told. She threatened if she ever found out that I was in contact with you again, she would make sure everyone knew the truth.' From that moment on, he said, 'I couldn't seem to get a few hours on my own no matter how hard I tried.'

"I patted Beefy's hand and told him the past was water under the bridge. He seemed grateful. Since my job was to keep him distracted, I got him started on the basketball stories again. In no time we were laughing and exchanging memories.

"Meanwhile in the bathroom, Darcy had pulled a bright red lipstick out of her pocket and painted her lips heavily. Then she slipped out of the bathroom and back into the kitchen. Quietly, she opened a half empty bottle of what I knew to be Beefy's favorite scotch. Then she poured two glasses full and poured a just a little in the other glass. She lifted one glass to her lips and put lipstick on the rim. She wet her fingertips and then placed the empty bottle on the counter beside the lid.

"Beefy still had his back to the kitchen door when Darcy returned and nodded to me. Then she casually walked up behind Beefy and rested her damp fingers on the back of Beefy's neck. She said we needed to be on our way since she had to work early tomorrow. She leaned over and kissed his cheek, thanking him for his hospitality. The bright lipstick stood out like a flag on a ski run against his pale skin.

"As we were gathering ourselves to leave, the front door opened, and the cackling of The Hens bustling in the door filled the room. Beefy looked at me and stiffened. There was actual fear in his eyes. We were in plain view of The Hens with no escape.

"The instant we were spotted, the voices stopped. The silence was deafening. At the front of the pack stood Bitsy, Beefy's wife. The fury emanated from her body in visible waves, contorting her rather plain face into something hideous. The focus of this rage was me.

The vein in her forehead pulsed and her hands were fisted on her narrow hips. I involuntarily took a few steps back.

"Then she began yelling. For a little woman, she was very loud when she bellowed at all of us, 'Don't any of you move!' She turned her murderous glare to Beefy. The sweat beads broke out on Beefy's forehead. He looked at his wife and began shaking his head. His lips moved but no sound came out. His little bitty wife strode over to him. She stood on tiptoe and smelled his neck, right near where Darcy had wiped his fingers. Then she reached up and wiped lipstick off his cheek. She looked at her fingers, then at Darcy and me and the lipstick on Darcy's lips.

"The sounds that came out of her then weren't really human. Think of the sound a hyena might make if a lion stole its meat. Then take the noise up about 5 notches. That's almost as angry-sounding as little Bitsy McGuire sounded that night. I don't think I ever heard that sound from a human being before. I felt Darcy's hand on my shoulder as she pushed me back toward the garage door. Bitsy stood on her tiptoes screaming at Beefy while The Hens stood transfixed just inside the front door.

"I felt cool air on my back. As I backed out, I saw Bitsy spring at Beefy, screaming and hitting and scratching. Beefy grabbed his wife's hands to stop her from hitting him. Poor Beefy kept saying he didn't do anything and begging me to tell her the truth. In that instant, she saw the empty bottle and the glasses on the counter. And I thought she'd been angry before! The sheer power of her increased rage could've launched a rocket ship.

"The Hens stepped inside far enough to see what was on the sink. The whole group gasped as one. Then they noticed we were almost out the door. One of them yelled, 'Oh no you don't!' The whole flock lifted their handbooks in the air, darted around the fighting couple and ran toward us. Darcy yelled, 'Run Scabby!'

"Now, running is out of the question for me these days, although I felt like I'd been required to skedaddle quite a bit since meeting Darcy a few weeks ago, but I shuffled as fast as I could. Fortunately, none of The Hens could move much faster. I looked over my shoulder and found an extra gear in my get-along when I saw the women coming as fast as they could behind me.

They had murder in their eyes and were intent on catching me. A couple of them were even using walkers, but they were gaining on me! I screamed at Darcy to start the car. I heard the car start and Darcy yell, "Hurry, they're going to catch you."

"I looked over my shoulder again, just in time to see a brown leather bag flash past my head. They were throwing things! I felt something hit my legs, and almost tripped. In my mind, I was running like Jessie Owens when he broke the world records in the 1936 Berlin Olympics. The unfortunate part of that delusion was that FloJo, Jackie Joyner-Kersee and Wilma Rudolph were all hot on my heels – and they were out for blood! In reality, all of us were shuffling as fast as our old legs would carry us and trying not to fall and break a hip.

"The only thing that saved me was Darcy. She'd gotten out of the car to come back to get me. She grabbed my arm and half-dragged me along. Just as she shoved me into the passenger side, The Hens caught up to us and began beating us with anything they had handy. Poor Darcy took the worst of the blows as she fought her way around the front to the driver's side.

"Those angry old women were swinging at her, screaming like banshees from the bowels of hell, and banging on the car, trying to get to us. They were spouting Bible quotes about drink and loose women and assuring us we were going straight to hell for tempting a good man like the preacher.

"Darcy had to carefully pull away from the curb as the crazy old biddies refused to give way. But the instant she was clear, she floored the car and raced down the street, careening around the first corner we came to. She looked in the rearview mirror at the group still shaking their fists and yelling at us. I leaned my head back and tried to calm my breathing.

"Darcy said, 'Wow.' I didn't look at her but said, 'Yeah.' Darcy heaved a sigh and said, 'That was brutal.' And, I added with a heavy sigh, 'Scary!'

"When we got home, Darcy and I spent an hour cleaning up cuts and scrapes and bruises. Darcy laughed and said that she never knew such nice old church ladies could be so mean. She hoped Beefy could handle the women on his own. I just shook my head and said that I wouldn't want to be him.

"A few days later, there was a newspaper article on the third page about how a retired local preacher who had gotten drunk and walked into the path of a cement truck early one morning. He'd been killed instantly. Darcy even looked sad when she showed me the article. The date was the morning after we had visited Beefy. Without saying anything, she took the list from her purse and crossed out my friend's name.

Frankie sniffed. I waited for the accusations, but they didn't come. "What?" I said, "You aren't going to blame me for this?" Frankie shook his head. "A good wife would have trusted the man she'd been married to for over 50 years and supported him."

He closed his laptop, muttered, "I'm never getting married!" and left.

Almost Brilliant

CHAPTER

21

At that point, there were only two people left between me and the big prize. I was beginning to think that this whole project might eventually be worth the price paid so far. I hated that three people had died but, like I kept telling Frankie, those deaths were not my fault. I even gave each of them a few moments of joy before they left this earth. I did not feel guilty. Darcy, though. Well, I was beginning to wonder about her. She seemed to actually be enjoying this a little too much.

When we got together to talk about what

happened to Beefy, she told me she was running out of money. The temp jobs weren't paying enough to stay in that house and the cash in SnotGun's wallet had only been a couple of hundred dollars. We were either going to have to hurry up or she was going to have to move into a box next to me and Maggie. I did not want her as an alley neighbor. I reminded her that we only had a few weeks left until the centennial.

Besides, Maggie was beginning to like staying over at the house. She got to sleep on the furniture, had fresh water whenever she wanted some and nice, warm cushions by the floor vent where she liked to sleep. I had tried not to get used to living like that but, well, I had to think of Maggie.

"A few days after Miss Faith's accident, I shed my nurse's clothes and went to the local diner to grab a bite. Dining out isn't something I do often, as one rarely knows what goes on in a public kitchen but, that day, I wanted to taste someone else's cooking for a change. I sat down in the least-tattered booth with my back to the room. I ran a hand across the vinyl tabletop and felt dampness like someone had done some recent cleaning. I smelled the slight odor of chlorine bleach. Knowing that someone had cleaned the table recently helped me relax a little. Shortly, a blonde waitress about my age, or a bit younger, came over with a cup of coffee and a menu. She took my order and asked if I needed anything else. I said I wanted to see the paper if there was one. A little light reading might turn up something interesting about this quiet little town.

"When the paper and my breakfast arrived, I glanced through the headlines. On the bottom of the first page was an article about the town's upcoming centennial celebration. There was a short history of the founding families and a list of the planned activities. The culminating event was the awarding of the grand prize to the oldest person in the town. The award was impressive. For a brief wistful moment, I wished I could qualify. Then I saw the list of the people in the running for the prize. The first two names were the two people who'd died on my watch, Creed Remington and Faith Chandler.

"But the last name on the list leapt out. Durwood "Scabby" Loudon. Where had I heard that name before? I kept on reading and letting the thought roll around in the back of my mind. As I finished my coffee and prepared to leave, I saw the scruffy little man who'd come to visit Mr. Remington a couple days before he died. He was on the other side of the street, sauntering past the bakery. I distinctly remembered not letting that dirty little man in to visit the clean sick room and the look on his face when I let him know that he wasn't welcome. In a brief instant, I wondered if he'd anything to do with the death of Mr. Remington or Miss Faith.

"My first instinct was to take this to the sheriff, but I had no solid evidence, only strong suspicions. Then I remembered the sheriff's reaction to my concerns. I was not sharing anything with that odious man until I had more proof. I was going to find out what was going on.

"After that day, I got into the habit of reading the local paper and having coffee at the dingy little diner every morning. The second day, I was reminded of one of the most amazing things about small towns. Everyone knows everything about everyone. And, if you know the local hot spot, all you have to do is sit quietly and listen. I heard about unfaithful husbands and who was having to refinance their house. Businesses in trouble, new babies coming, the medical test results ... everything was discussed out loud and in detail.

"A week or so after Miss Faith's accident, there was a page three article bemoaning the death of a well-loved local preacher. The report said the preacher had gone for a walk early one morning and accidently walked in front of a truck. He died instantly. I probably wouldn't have paid any attention except when I recognized his name from the list of potential award winners. Three of six dead within days of each other.

"The gossip was raging. The old ladies talked about how the preacher used to be a drinker but how his sainted mother and then his wife had gotten him away from the evil drink and back into the church. But, they whispered, the word was he was terribly intoxicated when he died. Someone else mentioned he probably started drinking again when he'd hooked up with that useless childhood friend of his. If anyone was to blame, they said, that bum Scabby was. One old lady stated loudly that Scabby was about as useless as a chocolate teapot. No one laughed.

My ears perked up at the mention of that name. Since I was sitting with my back to them in the next booth, I casually leaned back to listen more closely. But apparently, they had lost interest and were off to gossip about other topics, chattering like banty hens about nothing that interested me. A short while later, they gathered up their things and left as a single entity. The whole room seemed to heave a sigh of relief at their departure. When the waitress filled my cup again, I asked about the women. She filled me in on the group that she called The Hens and their role in the town. Then she added that I shouldn't pay a bit of attention to them. She said they often made-up stories when there was nothing else to talk about. 'So,' I asked, 'You don't believe what they are saying about the preacher and his friend?' The waitress looked away and then nervously pulled her pad out of her pocket and handed me my bill without another word. She disappeared into the kitchen seconds later.

"This mystery was getting more interesting by the day. This 'Scabby' person was now tied to another person on the list who had died mysteriously. And that waitress just might know more about the events than she was willing to talk about."

CHAPTER

Frankie came bounding into the cell early the next day. I'd never seen him so happy. Turned out he had passed all his exams despite his concerns. Now all he had to do was get through the last three months of classes and finals and he was a free man. I told him I was proud of him for doing something I hadn't been able to do.

"Why didn't you ever go back and, at least, get your GED?" he asked.

"Well, mostly because all I ever cared about was making enough money to have food, a roof and alcohol, not always in that order," I added, "on a regular basis and the company of a lady once in a while." I sighed and said, "I honestly never thought I'd live this long." I told him about a song I heard once that said a person should die young and leave a purty corpse. "I thought I would do just that," I said. He couldn't help grinning.

"What?" I gasped. "You don't think I'm purty?"

He shook his head, his smile spreading.

"Well, young man," I said haughtily, "Enough ladies did in my day so who cares what you think." We both laughed at that!

That kind of brought me to the next person on the list. I settled into my little nest of pillow, guided Maggie into my lap and began to fill him in. Miss Savannah Layton was a beautiful girl, even in grade school. Of course, that wasn't much of a surprise since her momma, Miss Kayla Layton, was on the beauty queen circuit from the time she was a child. I told him I had heard she competed all the way to the last round of the Miss USA pageant but came in second. Her mother, Miss Glory Layton, was one of those not-quite beautiful women who try to live her dreams through her child. She pushed her daughter to be perfect all the time. Only the best was good enough for Miss Glory. People told stories about her browbeating Miss Kayla for the tiniest things; dusty shoes on a hot summer day, damp shirt after being rained on, not speaking clearly enough, speaking too loudly, any number of things.

"Rumor was that at the Miss USA pageant, Miss Kayla was so upset about being second that she attacked the winner and Miss Glory jumped out of the audience and attacked the judges on national television. They were both hauled away in hand cuffs. Miss Glory, of course, blamed Miss Kayla for the failure and locked her in the big old house when they came home.

"The next week, Miss Kayla was spirited away to stay with relatives, according to the housekeeper who cooked for the Layton women. Miss Kayla came back home six months later with a detailed story about a cousin and her husband being killed in a car accident and how, just before she died, the woman had begged Miss Kayla to raise the child. Being the good Christian women they were, Miss Glory agreed to let the baby live with them.

"Everyone knew that was a lie, but no one was brave enough to cross that harridan. Mother and daughter disappeared with the baby into the decrepit house venturing out only when needed. Until one day when Miss Kayla was found wandering the streets late at night, dressed in one of her pageant gowns and a tiara. She seemed to have no idea how she had gotten there. The police took her home and handed her off to a furiously embarrassed Miss Glory. The next day, she just disappeared. People guessed she was over in some hospital in another state just so Miss Glory would not have to see her. No one asked about her for fear of angering the old woman.

"Of course, not long after Miss Kayla left, that old biddy saw another chance at her dream in baby Savannah and pushed her down the same beauty pageant road. Miss Savannah was the spitting image of her mother. Miss Glory dressed her in same frilly dresses that she had dressed Miss Kayla in every day. She raised Miss Savannah, as strictly as she had her daughter. The child wasn't allowed to play or run or do any normal kid things. Miss Glory watched that child as closely as if there were gypsies on every corner waiting to steal her away.

"I met Miss Savannah when she came to first grade late in the year. Much later, I heard that the grandmother had been forced to send her to school. I just remember seeing a perfect doll standing in the front of the class with a shaky smile pasted on her face. She looked like she should be under glass or in a store window somewhere. Before long, everyone could tell she knew nothing about counting or writing or anything the rest of the class knew, but she could pose and walk perfectly. She sang little songs whenever asked to, but other than that she stayed to herself. She didn't appear to be mentally challenged but, rather, she seemed like a beautiful robot, for she responded when asked, but did nothing on her own.

Frankie said that must have been a terrible childhood for her. I nodded and said, "I guess." She never talked to anyone and she was out of school a lot. Even years after she was gone from school, her beauty was the topic of gossip for many jealous girls. We found out in middle school that the days she'd missed were because she'd been competing in pageants all over the country just like her mother had.

"The other memory I have of Miss Savannah was the last day she was in school; the day she started screaming in class and wouldn't stop. We were sitting at our desks doing writing ... must have been second grade. While the rest of us were learning to write sentences and punctuation, Miss Savannah was still forming letters and trying to recognize small words. The classroom was quiet as everyone worked.

"Suddenly, as if bitten by a rattlesnake, Miss Savannah bolted out of her chair and started screaming. Not just a scream, but a blood-curdling terrified might-be-ready-to-die scream. Several other girls started screaming too, but they stopped when they realized there was no apparent danger. Miss Savannah, however, stood staring at her paper like the page had turned into some sort of fierce creature.

"The stunned teacher raced over and tried to comfort her, but Miss Savannah wouldn't even let the teacher touch her. She kept pointing at the paper and screaming. The petrified teacher sent a student to the office who brought the principal racing in. He tried to help, but nothing would calm her. Then, as suddenly as she'd started screaming, she crumpled to the floor. The rest of us were terrified. We thought Miss Savannah had died. The principal scooped her up and carried her out of the classroom while the teacher tried to get us all back to work. Once we were settled, the teacher gathered up Miss Savannah's paper and stared at the unsteady handwriting, shaking her head and muttering that she couldn't see what was wrong.

"A few days later, I was in the office fighting – again – and I heard one of the ladies behind the counter tell the other that Miss Savannah wouldn't be coming back. The first one shook her head and said, 'All this mess because she made a mistake forming a letter.'

"'So that was what set her off,' I thought.

Frankie blew out breath in a soft whistle. "I know," I said. "To this day, I remember her screaming and cannot figure what old Miss Glory had done to her in order to make her fear such a little mistake so much."

"So, what happened to her?" Frankie asked.

"Miss Glory and Miss Savannah just walled themselves up in that old house. When Miss Glory died, officials realized the main building was about to fall in on itself so the town decided to condemn the structure. Miss Savannah was forced to move into the much smaller caretaker's cottage on the edge of the property, closer to town but still by itself. There were church ladies that went up and cleaned for her occasionally. They said she was always dressed like she was going to attend some fancy-dress ball. But now her dresses were tattered and torn and her hair and makeup weren't as good since she lost her sight.

"Lost her sight?" Frankie gasped. "How did that happen?"

"Not sure," I mused. "No one is. The church ladies found her lying in the middle of her kitchen floor one afternoon. They called an ambulance that brought her to the hospital. She had a big lump on the side of her head. I guess she fell and damaged her eyes somehow."

Shortly thereafter, we finished up for the day. Frankie had some things he had to do for his mom, and I had some thinking to do.

CHAPTER

When Frankie returned, I told him about the plan Darcy, Maggie and I had come up with. Darcy'd done some poking around and found out which church had sent people in to clean for Miss Savannah. She also found out that Miss Savannah loved roses. She had pots of them all over her house, inside and out, all year round and even hired a local nursery to come and care for them. In the spring, they came and transplanted and pollenated the pots. Someone went over weekly to water and check on the plants.

"'That seems like a lot of money to spend on plants,' I said. Darcy said that Miss Savannah was financially well off from the pageant money her mother had made and the sale of some land. She could afford to have people come in if she wanted to. She looked at me and raised her eyebrows. I got the unstated meaning immediately. Savanah didn't need the prize as much as I did.

"She had also found out one other important detail. Miss Savannah suffered from melissophobia: fear of bees. She looked at me so pointedly that I was afraid her eyebrows would fly right off her face. I looked back at her, wondering what her devilish mind had come up with this time. "Are you thinking what I'm thinking?" she asked.

"I doubt I am," I said. She scoffed and looked down at Maggie. "How do you put up with this?" she asked. Maggie just stared at her and pulled her upper lip back in her famous smile. 'She loves me,' I said. 'Good thing someone does,' Darcy teased. 'Here is what I am thinking....' Darcy went on to outline a plan.

Frankie looked at me with accusation in his eyes when I looked at him. He said, "If you tell me, you put bees in her house, which counts as murder." I waved my hands and said "No, that wasn't the plan at all."

Darcy said that since Miss Savannah was so sweet and had had such a tough life, she just wanted to scare her into leaving town. She reminded me that we didn't have much time. I followed her thinking. This plan would take more time and preparation than the others had demanded. I wasn't sure all that work was going to pay off at all. Darcy said all we had to do was to figure out the schedule of people who visited her and plan to be there on a free day, if there was one. I said I'd have to think on this plan. I looked at Maggie. She looked back but did not sneeze.

"Darcy said we had to put the plan in action the next week, so I needed to clear my head quickly. She was going to spend the day putting together some stuff she thought we needed, and I should come out to her house that evening so we could plan further. I told her I would and left. I talked to Maggie as we walked home about the plan, but she ignored me completely. She walked a little behind me and her tail was not flying as high as usual. I was beginning to think this was not a good idea.

Frankie laughed and said, "So far Maggie has given you the go ahead on everything that worked. Maybe you should have listened to her," he added. I reached out and patted Maggie's little furry head. She groaned in her sleep. I told Frankie he was so right!

"When I went back to Darcy's place, she was sitting at the kitchen table with a small tape recorder in front of her. She seemed to be listening intently to something playing on the tape. I couldn't hear a sound. She looked up and put a finger to her lips. I sat down as quietly as I could and listened. I still couldn't hear anything except for Maggie on the floor next to me, twisted her head side to side like she was listening to music. We sat there for a few minutes. Darcy shut the tape recorder off and pushed the black box toward me. 'What did you hear?' she asked.

"I told her she'd have to turn the sound up. All I could hear was a bunch of buzzing. 'That's what you should hear,' she said. 'That is the sound of bees!' I reached over, turned on the player and listened again. Sure enough, the tape was nothing but the sound of buzzing bees.

"'How did you do that?' I asked. Darcy said, 'Well, I've been, pardon the pun, a busy little bee. Did you know there was an apiary out south of town?' I shook my head. 'Well, the cook at the diner told me he gets fresh honey from there. So, I drove out this afternoon and took my tape recorder with me. I told the bee farmer that I was from the university and I was studying the sounds bees make. I was trying to see if different hives make different sounds and how many different types of buzzing I could discover.' I pursed my lips in surprise. "Good idea,' I said. 'Great idea!' she said with enthusiasm and punched my shoulder.

"I rubbed my shoulder and told her not to do that again. She said, 'Ok how about this?' She handed me the sleep mask that she used when she had to work nights and told me to put the mask on and pull the straps tightly. I reluctantly did as she asked. 'Now just sit still and listen,' she said. I heard the sound of the bees buzzing softly at first; then louder and louder. The sound seemed to get closer. With the mask on, the buzzing sounded like there were hundreds of bees in the room.

"Then I felt something poke me. More than a poke, there was a soft feathery touch and then a sharp little poke on my neck. Instinctively, I slapped the area. I was tickled and poked on the other side of my neck, then on my arm and my cheek. The sound of the bees grew still louder. I knew for fact that there were no bees in the house, but my ears were telling me otherwise, and, two against one, they were winning the argument against my brain. And my skin was siding with my ears.

"When I couldn't stand it any longer, I snatched off the mask and opened my eyes. There stood Darcy grinning broadly. In each of her hands was a small wooden dowel with tiny feathers and stick pins taped to the end of them. She started laughing and said, 'Tell me that didn't feel like you were being attacked by bees!'

"I said the sensation felt very real. Even though, I knew there were no bees in here, I was convinced I was being stung. 'Is this what we are going to do to Ms. Savannah?' She said, 'Yes.' 'How will that take her out of the running,' I asked. Darcy said I'm hoping the sound and the feeling like she is being stung will scare her to death and she will just drop over right there in her tracks!' 'Darcy!' I yelled at her. 'How can you be so heartless?'

"She sat down beside me and took my hands. 'I'm doing this for us, Scabby, for you. We need this prize. Otherwise, I'm going to have to go back to the city and start stripping again and you're going to have to sleep in that cold, wet box until the day you die.'

"'I dropped my shoulders. I couldn't argue with her. 'Besides,' she said, 'we've already come so far. All our effort shouldn't be wasted.' I pulled my hands back and put them on my knees. I looked at Maggie who jumped up and put her paws on my knees and licked my hand. I decided that was as good as a sneeze. 'Ok,' I said.

CHAPTER

24

"When I met Darcy at the diner the next afternoon, she handed me a piece of paper with my coffee. She'd drawn a month calendar on the paper. There were notes in most of the blocks. She said, 'That's the schedule of when people visited Miss Savannah. Today is here.' She put her finger on a square. The square had the word 'flowers' written in the middle and the next square said 'cleaning'. 'You see,' she said, 'there are two days a week no one visits. One of those days is when we choose to visit Miss Savannah.' I looked at the calendar, still not quite believing we were going to do this. 'What is this one with the cross?' I asked. Darcy shook her head and said, 'She has a monthly appointment of some kind. She's usually gone all day. Someone picks her up, takes her away for the day and then drops her off again late in the afternoon.' The following square was empty, and that pattern repeated all month.

"'By the way,' Darcy said, 'did you know she is still in contact with the cousins her mother went to visit?' I said, 'No, I thought she was alone in the world.' Darcy shook her head again and said, 'The woman who cleans her house came into the diner yesterday while she was there and told her coffee pals about Miss Savannah being excited about her relatives coming to spend the weekend. The cleaner was grousing because she had spent two extra hours making up the spare room.'

"Darcy added, 'She said something odd though.' I looked at her quizzically. 'She said that she hoped the nursery people who took care of Miss Savannah's roses had enough plants in stock. Everyone at the table had laughed loudly at that comment.' 'Huh,' I said, 'I wonder what that means. Didn't you say she had tons of roses in her place?' Darcy quipped, 'I guess we'll find out.'

Frankie sniffed. "What's with you?" I asked.

"Roses!" he said, "I have allergies!"

I smirked and said, "You wouldn't have had a problem with these roses!" He looked quizzically at me.

"I'll get to the point," I promised. "Be patient. Shall I go on?" He nodded and poised those long fingers over the board again.

I went back to the story. "I looked at Darcy's calendar again. I scratched my head and said, "The next time she goes out for the day is tomorrow. Why don't we go and scope the place out a bit this time?' Darcy tipped her head to the right and said, 'I think that's a fine idea. I'll call in sick and we'll go about ten.' I nodded and finished my coffee.

"The next day, she ready right on time and we drove out to see where Miss Savannah lived. Maggie was out of the car first, racing around, trying to smell everything. Darcy and I walked directly up to the house. The first thing that we noticed was that there wasn't a rose bush on the property. I asked, 'I thought you said there were roses everywhere.' 'That's what the cleaning lady said,' Darcy answered. 'I guess that's why she always did air quotes when she said roses and laughed. I think Miss Savannah is being taken advantage of here,' Darcy observed. I had to agree.

"There were no cars in the drive, but we slipped along the hedges up to the house and looked in the window. The house was full of light, neat and uncluttered. I couldn't see a sign of anyone there. I whispered to Darcy, 'What are those things? They look like big funeral urns.' Darcy answered loudly, 'First, why are we whispering? There is no one here.' I nodded sheepishly at that. 'Second,' she said in a normal tone, 'let's see if we can get in and find out.' We walked around to the front door. Maggie guided us, her tail flying high. The wooden door was heavy and locked. We looked in the windows alongside the door, trying to think of another way in. Suddenly, Maggie woofed and took off around the corner. A few seconds later, she was looking at us from inside the house, smiling her doggy smile. I looked at Darcy and we went in the direction Maggie had gone. There was a smaller less substantial door about halfway down the wall. That door was locked as well but there was a good-sized pet door at the bottom. I wondered briefly what that was for since she had no pets that we knew of.

"Darcy sat down on the stone steps, leaned against the door, lifted the plastic flap and reached inside up to her shoulder. She strained, trying to reach the lock, but finally pulled her arm back out. 'My arm's not long enough,' she said. 'I'm sure I cannot fit through that door, so you're going to have to.' 'Me?' I gasped. 'Yes, you!' She said in a threatening tone. 'You are skinnier than me. Now, get down here.'

"I slowly sank down beside her and looked at that pet door. Now, I'm not the biggest guy in the world, but that door wasn't very big either. I figured a good-sized cocker spaniel cold keep in easily. Darcy urged, 'If you put your head and shoulders through and then drag yourself in as far as you can, you'll be able to twist your hips sideways enough to slip through.' I shook my head, but she grabbed me by the shoulder and pushed me toward the little opening. Then she demanded, 'Get in there. I'll be right here to help.'

"I guess you could call what she did helping. I took my jacket off and handed it to her to hold and then lifted the weather flap. Maggie looked at me from the other side, tail waving happily. She dropped her front quarters to the floor as if inviting me to play. I told her that this wasn't the time, but she didn't listen. I stuck my head and arms in and began to wiggle my way inside.

Maggie was so excited to see me down on her level that she raced over and began to cover me with kisses. I pushed her away a couple times until she finally got the hint and sat down a few feet away from me. She watched me with reproach in her eyes.

"When I was up to my shoulders, Darcy started trying to help tuck me through the door. 'Ow! That hurts,' I yelled, but my shoulders slipped inside. I worked hard to pull myself in farther. As predicted when I got to my hips, the door was a tighter squeeze. Again, I felt her trying to fold me into the opening like tucking a too-short shirttail into a pair of tight pants without undoing the belt. 'Stop that!' I yelled. 'I'm helping,' she insisted, 'Pull yourself through!' Then she grabbed my legs and twisted and pushed hard as hard as she could. I plopped into the kitchen. Maggie ran over to congratulate me! I was just pleased to have finished the ordeal alive and still wearing my pants!

"I pulled my legs in and turned around to

see Darcy looking in the flap. 'Open the door,' she ordered. 'Give me a minute,' I groused at her. 'I feel like I've just been birthed. I hate you right now.' I lay on the floor a few minutes longer. My poor hips felt like an elephant had sat on me. Then, to add insult to injury, Maggie popped out and back in the door like a cork from a champagne bottle and sat next to me, wagging her tail and smiling at me. She looked happy to be playing this game. I told her to shut up and struggled to my feet. She danced out of the way and started exploring the room.

"All over the floor were bowls holding dry cat food. Maggie wandered around, helping herself to several of them joyfully.

I looked over at Frankie. His head was hunched down and his shoulders were shaking. "What's with you," I asked. He lifted a hand toward me in a gesture that said stop. Then he giggled like a little kid. Then he sat up straight, held his sides and laughed.

"I," he stammered through the gales of laughter, "have this, ha ha, image in my head of you, ha ha, stuck in that door and Darcy, ha ha, pushing... and Maggie, ha ha..." By then, he was laughing so hard that tears were streaming down his face.

"Go ahead," I sulked. "Yuck it up. You'll be laughing out the other side of your face soon enough. Get your pleasure over my pain over with but know that right now I hate you!" He nodded but kept on laughing. He laughed for so long that I finally told him to take Maggie for a walk until he got himself under control. He walked down the hall, giggling under his breath. For a terrible moment, I was afraid he would stop in the office and tell the sheriff and deputies the story. I listened with bated breath for the sound of roaring laughter in the lobby, but none came. I was grateful the kid kept his mouth shut! First, because if he told the sheriff and deputies, the story would be all over town by noon. I would never live that story down. And second, that escapade was part of what I didn't want anyone else to know yet.

When he came back, his face was tinged red and he was still smiling. I said, sarcasm dripping, "are you ready now?" He smiled and nodded. "No more giggling," I demanded. He nodded his head but the smile didn't leave. "Thank you for not telling the guys out front." He replied, his voice barely controlled, "I had a hard time not telling them."

"Okay. Enough laughter at my expense," I ordered. "Let's move on.

"As soon as we got into the house, Darcy looked at all the dishes on the floor. 'She must feed half the cats in the county.' We walked in the living room and we understood what the air quotes with the word 'roses' was all about. The scent of roses was heavy in the air and there were lots of decorative flower pots – what I thought were funeral urns – around the room. But those

277

pots contained only a few ugly, very dusty plastic roses. A wad of yellow-stained cotton was glued at the top of each flower. 'What in the world, I asked, do you think this is?'

"Darcy looked around and picked up a small glass bottle from a shelving unit beside the door. The label said 'attar of roses'. She showed the little brown bottle to me and gestured around the room. She said, 'This explains the smell. Dabbing this oil concentrate on the cotton once in a while would make a blind person think there were roses here and the nursery would be able to charge her for caring for the roses while actually doing nothing.'

"I was furious for Miss Savannah, thinking that no one deserved to be treated like that. Then I remembered why we were here. 'I guess she doesn't touch them at all,' I said.

"'The nursery that had been hired to take care of the roses really better be ordering lots of roses this week if her relatives are coming to visit,' Darcy smirked. We spent a few minutes wandering around and planning our routes. Maggie sat in the middle of the living room and watched us. When we were ready to leave, I asked her what she thought. She sneezed, but I think the scent of all the fake roses caused her to do that this time.

"We had two days to practice our plan. We took turns being the bees and being Miss Savannah so we could get good at tickling and poking just right. Darcy thought we should go back out to the bee farm and deliberately anger the bees so we could feel the sting. I drew the line at that!

Frankie stopped me. "Did you really believe this was going to work?" I nodded. "To some extent, yes, but honestly, I wasn't sure how this one would end. There was a lot to figure out which meant a lot to go wrong."

"Our biggest problem was getting in the door," I told him. "I certainly couldn't be rebirthed quietly enough not to disturb her with her in the house. Darcy decided she'd think of a reason to be invited into the house and get the door opened that way. Then I could sneak in behind her. That way, she explained, she could pretend like she was being attacked as well if she needed to and that would add to the reality of the plan." I agreed. I still wasn't sure this idea would work but what did we have to lose? But that clever Darcy came up with a perfect plan that did away with the need for me to reenact the birthing process or for her to have to pretend to be attacked.

"We went to the house the next time Miss Savannah's calendar said she'd be alone. Darcy knocked on the door. When Miss Savannah answered, Darcy introduced herself as Mrs. Andrea Jones and said she was a county census taker who needed a few minutes of her time. Miss Savannah let her in without a second's hesitation. I followed in stockinged feet and waited in the kitchen for my cue.

"The first thing I noticed was that the ugly cotton and plastic flowers had been replaced by some scrawny, but real, rose bushes. None of them had natural flowers on them since it wasn't their blooming season, but whoever had replaced the plants had stuck the cotton balls down into the dirt, so the smell was still there.

"I stood by the kitchen island and let the two women get settled into chairs in the adjoining living room. Darcy pulled the tape player out of her bag, placed the little black box on the table as quietly as she could and then pulled out a clip board. Darcy said she loved all the flowers. Miss Savannah thanked her and told her about her love for the smell of roses. She replied that she preferred to have the plants inside. It was easier and safer than having them outside. Darcy asked if her blindness made her afraid of going outside.

Miss Savannah wrapped her arms around herself and shook her head. She whispered, 'I'm afraid of the bees.' 'Bees?' Darcy questioned. Miss

Savannah nodded and told her that when she was a child visiting a cousin's house, one of the neighborhood kids had accidentally disturbed a wild beehive in a log and the bees had swarmed on him. 'He died right there in the yard – covered in hideous red bumps – before they could get him help. I didn't lose my sight until a few years ago,' she said. 'I remember what things look like and some of them I wish I could forget. That is certainly one of them.'

"Darcy patted her knee and reached over to the tape player. The sound could barely be heard, but Miss Savanah noticeably stiffened. Darcy began asking questions about how many people lived in the house. Miss Savannah's voice quivered slightly as she answered. Then she leaned toward Darcy and whispered, 'Can you hear that?' Darcy said she didn't hear anything at all and asked another question about the size of the house itself. She asked several more questions about the house and the area, turning up the sound slightly after each one. Miss Savannah more alert with every increase in the sound, but she remained statue-like, gripping the chair's arms and answered each question quietly with a quavering voice.

"Darcy waved me into the living room and I slipped up behind Miss Savannah. Darcy turned up the tape player a bit more and Miss Savannah shivered. 'Are you sure you can't hear that?' Ms. Savannah whimpered. 'I don't hear anything, Honey,' Darcy said. 'Are you OK?'

"Miss Savannah bobbed her head tentatively. 'Don't worry,' Darcy said soothingly, 'I used to work as a nurse. If anything happens, I'm here for you but I really don't hear anything.' She looked up and winked at me. I gave her a half-smile and she continued, 'Is there any medicine you should be taking or anyone I can call?' Miss Savannah shook her head and said, 'Maybe I am just tired. Could we finish this another time?' she asked. Darcy patted her hand and said, 'There are only couple more questions. Maybe I should get you some water.'

"That was my clue to poke Miss Savannah softly. She shrieked and jumped up, slapping at the place on her arm where I'd poked her. Darcy stood up and pulled her sticks out of the huge bag, and said, 'Miss Layton, what is wrong?' Darcy reached down and turned up the noise further. Then both of us began poking Miss Savannah with all four sticks, being careful to keep away from her slapping hands. She was frozen in place but slapped at her body while screaming and begging Darcy to help her. Darcy kept asking if she was ok and what was wrong, but Miss Savannah was too frightened to answer. I felt terrible, but Darcy gave me the stink eye, so I kept on.

"After a few seconds of the torture, Miss Savannah dropped back into her chair. She reached down into a drawer under the table beside her chair and pulled out a huge can of wasp spray. She jumped up and screamed while turning in circles, spraying the poison in every direction. Darcy was quicker than me. She ducked out of the way, but I'd been standing right in front of Miss Savannah and, before I could react, she sprayed the poison right in my face. I fell backward a step or two, trying not to gasp or yell but couldn't hold back a small choking cough.

"Miss Savannah turned toward me and yelled, 'Who is there?' 'It's just me, Miss Layton. Mrs. Jones,' Darcy stepped in front of her and took the can from Miss Savannah. 'Is there someone else here?' Miss Savannah demanded. 'No,' Darcy said, 'Honey, you're just too excited and imagining things. A few seconds later, Miss Savannah seemed to wilt like one of her roses and plopped into her chair again. Her head lolled back, and her eyes closed.

"I stumbled to the door and ran into the yard coughing and choking. Then Darcy ran after me to be sure I was OK. I asked if Savannah was dead but Darcy said she'd checked for a pulse. Miss Savannah's was strong, but she was out cold. Darcy told me to stay there and she darted back in to clean everything up. She left me trying to get the smell of the bug spray out of my lungs, the sting out of my watering eyes and the taste out of my mouth. When she returned, handed me a dish towel that she'd grabbed and soaked in water. I wiped my eyes, nose and mouth as we half ran, half fell toward the car.

"Darcy scampered back to the house once more to be sure she'd gathered up all our things. She said she'd heard Miss Savannah screaming into the phone calling 911. By the time we heard sirens coming, my eyes had stopped burning a bit and I could breathe again. Darcy started up the car and we drove out calmly as you please.

"So," Frankie interjected, "You didn't kill her at all then." "Nope," I said, "Just left her there alive and well. If the cops hadn't come soon, we'd have called them. I was the only one who was punished that day."

"Good," he said, "You deserved what happened to you." I snorted and continued my story.

"The next day Darcy was in the diner when a group of EMTs were, talking about how they'd gone out and found Miss Savannah nearly out of her mind. They said she was running around with an empty can of wasp spray, trying to spray more poison, screaming about the house being full of bees and asking for the census taker who could prove she was telling the truth. But there were no bees, no open windows, and no other people, nothing in the house at all. They thought Miss Savannah might be losing her mind like her momma did before her. Because the smell of bug spray was so strong, they took her to the hospital to be checked out and held overnight. When she woke up the next day, she refused to go back to her house. Darcy seemed quite pleased with the way things had turned out."

I told Frankie that Darcy and I had planned

to go out again when Miss Savannah was back home and do the whole act all over again, but this time I'd be some kind of repair man checking on something for the city. But there was no need.

Frankie jumped up, "Yes!" he said, "You finally grew a conscience and let the poor woman be, right?" I shook my head. "We didn't have to do anything at all." Frankie sat back down, tipped his head to the left like Maggie did when she was trying to understand something and waited for me to continue.

"That weekend her relatives came and swept her away. No one knew if she'd called them or if they came on the scheduled visit a couple days earlier than planned. The cleaning ladies said that two days after the ambulance was called out there, their cleaning services were cancelled after one last time. All accounts for all the utilities were closed and a big moving truck pulled up to the gate. Miss Savannah left without a forwarding address or anything. Apparently, the relatives had found some ugly plastic flowers in the house. The flowers were left in the house with a scathing note condemning anyone who'd take advantage of a blind person that way."

"But," he said, "She was out of the way just the same, right?" I nodded. "Only one left to go!"

CHAPTER

25

"The next time I visited the diner, the gossips were abuzz with news about a woman I'd seen in the ER two nights before. When she was admitted, she had been terrified. Relatives had swooped in and moved her lock stock and barrel out of the town without telling anyone where they were taking her. Of course, the town's talkers thought her leaving was a good thing. She should never have been living out there all alone anyway, especially if she was losing her mind like her momma had. I thought back to my conversation with her the morning after she'd been brought in.

"She looked pale and wan when I arrived, but she was definitely not out of her mind. I wasn't in uniform, so I introduced myself and told her I'd been in the ER when they brought her to the hospital. I was worried about her and wanted to see if I could help in any way. She faced the window and didn't respond for a few minutes. 'Do you know where you are?' I asked. She nodded. 'Has anyone explained the room to you?' I laid a gentle hand on her hand. She turned her hand over and grabbed mine tightly.

"'Tell me,' she said. 'Tell you what?' I asked. 'How bad do I look?' she cried softly. 'My dear,' I said as kindly as I could, 'you look fine.' Sobs burst out of her in a torrent. I handed her a tissue and waited for the spasm to wind down. I sat on the edge of her bed and said, 'Now tell me why you would think you looked bad.'

"She told me about a childhood incident with a boy who'd died of bee stings and how she

291

still had her sight then. As I'd seen someone in full anaphylactic shock more than once, I could understand how such a memory would be terrifying for her. Then she continued, 'All I can see in my mind is him covered with angry red welts and his tongue swelling up so big that it wouldn't fit in his mouth anymore.' The sobs started all over again. I sat forward and pulled her into my arms I waited until she cried herself dry and then laid her back on the pillow. I took my time and went over her neck, face, arms and legs looking for stings. I noticed some odd little scratches on her arms and a few very small reddish dots on her face and neck, but nothing like what a bee sting would look like. I told her my findings and she visibly relaxed. She apologized for being so out of control. I shushed her and said from what she told me I'd have been more worried if she was in control. She smiled. I asked her if she wanted to tell me what happened at her house.

"After a couple of sips of water, she told

me about the census taker who'd come to ask her questions. Right then, I realized something was wrong, as this was not a census year. But I didn't stop her. She said the woman came in, sat down and started asking her questions. Almost as soon as she started, Miss Savannah said she heard buzzing, very quiet and soft. She said she asked if the woman could hear anything, but the woman said she couldn't. She kept on asking questions, and the buzzing kept getting louder and louder. Miss Savannah hugged herself at the memory. 'I couldn't even focus on the questions,' she said, 'but the woman kept saying there was nothing there.'

"I clenched my jaw at the thought of the fear this gentle creature had gone through. But something wasn't ringing true. I couldn't put a name to my concern, but I would. Sooner or later, I would. Then she shivered and continued, 'I started feeling bees stinging me. They were everywhere. I grabbed the wasp and bee spray out from under the table and started spraying in every direction. The woman grabbed me and told me I was imagining things, but by that time I was so scared that I fell into my chair. I might have passed out for a minute or two. When I sat up, I called her name, but no one was there, so I went to the phone and called 911.'

"'She was gone?' I asked. 'Yes, I thought that was odd,' Miss Savannah added, 'for a moment, I almost began to believe I'd imagined her too, but I know I didn't. The men who came said there were no bees, all the windows were closed and even the door was locked. They said no one else was there and they'd had to break a pane of glass to get in, so the doors were locked from the inside.'

"I saw the tears well up in her eyes again. 'Maybe,' she whispered, 'I'm just a crazy old woman like my mother. She lost her mind when I was little and died in an institution years later. I remember my grandmother telling me stories about her and her crazy ways. Maybe my turn has come.'

"I assured her she seemed quite sane to me. I told her I didn't understand what had happened either, but possibly this census person had done something. 'But why?' Ms. Savannah wondered, 'Why would she want to hurt me?' I had no answer for her. I suggested she lie back and rest. I told her where the water pitcher and drinking glass were. I asked if there was anyone, I could call for her. She said she'd already called her relatives. She was too scared to go home, and they'd been asking her to come and live with them for years. This was just the last straw. She was finally going to live with them for good.

"I started to leave, when she said that she'd just remembered another odd thing. I walked back to the bed and waited for her to go on. She said, 'I almost think there was someone else there.' 'Really?' I asked. 'Why?' 'Well, when I was spraying the wasp spray around, I heard someone gasp and cough right in front of me, but

I could hear the woman was behind me telling me to calm down.' Her face screwed up into a frown. 'Isn't that odd?'

"Odd indeed, I thought. I just wondered who that other person might have been."

Almost Brilliant

CHAPTER

The next day Darcy's had a day off. We met at the diner for breakfast. As usual, we sat at a window table in the diner as far away from others as we could get. We talked over what had happened with Miss Savannah and Darcy pulled out her list to scratch the name off. She looked at the last name and circled the letters. Then, instead of putting the list back in her purse like always, she pushed the piece of paper across the table to me.

"You are going to have to do this last one

alone," she said. I frowned and waited for her to continue. "I got a call from a friend in the city," she said. "I have to go there for a while."

I was shocked. I told her that we'd been a great team on this project. I kinda thought she'd hang around and reap the reward. She shook her head. "I'd like to but this friend needs me. He has always been there for me and I need to be there for him."

"Ohh," I said letting my eyebrows raise in interest.

"No," she scoffed, "not that kind of friend. When Momma died, he helped me through the long dark days and now he has been diagnosed with an illness. He wouldn't tell me what was wrong on the phone so I don't know how long I'll be gone."

She reached across the table and placed her hand on top of mine. "I liked this time, Scabby, a lot more than I thought I would. You just win the prize – the announcement's only a week away –

and get all set up. As soon as my friend is out of the woods, I'll come back to see you."

I could feel my eyes sting a bit. That this woman had come to mean so much to me in so short a time amazed me. But I nodded and asked when she was leaving. She glanced out the window. Her car was parked at the curb, packed to the top with her things.

"Listen," she said, "the rent is paid on the house until the end of the month. If you want, I'll ask the landlord if you can stay there until then."

I shook my head. If I was going to have to go back to my box, I might as well make a clean break. I thanked her and said, "Nah. Maggie and I made sure we never got used to that soft life, like clean sheets and hot water and stuff. We'll be fine. You just go ahead and do what you have to do." I was lying out my teeth. I was going to hate giving up all that comfort. The idea of going back to my box made me resolve to finish the job. I didn't want to spend the rest of my life climbing in and out of that box.

"OK," she said and slapped a five-dollar bill on the table. She pulled an envelope out of her enormous purse and slid the packet across the table to me. "That has my phone number, where I'll be and some things, I want you to have. Keep it somewhere safe in case you need me." I nodded and she continued, "I'll get on my way then."

We stood up and walked to the door. Beside the car, Darcy leaned down and patted Maggie on the head and told her to keep me clean. Maggie looked up at her and sneezed three times in row. We laughed. Then she hugged me and said, "I'm gonna miss you ... Dad."

That almost did me in. I have heard that you never know what you have until you've lost it, but I'm here to say that sometimes you don't know what you've been missing until it arrives either. I never had a family or even wanted a family. I'd seen all the trouble and heartache others went through because of the people that were supposed to love and care for them, but that little word whispered from her lips made me wish I had the last forty plus years to do over.

Just before she got in the car, she said, "By the way, that last guy on the list has an aneurysm in his brain. A bunch of nurses came in for coffee yesterday when I was there for lunch," she smiled slyly. "Apparently, they don't like him much. He has been ordered to stay as calm as he can. The doctors are afraid if he gets too excited about anything, the bubble will burst and he'll die." She looked at me meaningfully. I got the drift right away. She started to slide into the car, rose up one more time and winked. "Oooo, and this week's lottery is $6 million. Pretty exciting, huh?"

CHAPTER

27

"I came in early and pretended to do chart work. Sitting at the back desk looking busy was the surest way to make certain no one interrupted me. I logged in to the hospital system and checked to see if Miss Layton was still in her room, but she had been released.

"On a whim, I looked up the name 'Scabby'. I found a long history for one Durwood P. Loudon. Working backward, I found he'd recently been in the ER with severe gastro-intestinal distress. I checked the date. I wasn't surprised when I found that day was the same date that Faith Chandler had had her accident. I looked at his record and saw that the person who brought him in said he'd eaten what he thought was a chocolate bar but turned out to be a laxative that looked like chocolate called Ex-lax. I filed that away for later thinking.

CHAPTER

28

Frankie showed up a couple days later empty-handed, looking unhappy and uncomfortable. I let him settle down and asked him what was wrong. He said that his parents thought he was spending too much time here and the newspaper editor said he was tired of waiting. If he didn't have a story by Monday, he was going to cancel the space.

I sighed and said, "Ok, then we better get this project finished." He said he would come back the next day with his laptop. I promised to be ready to go.

When he returned, I told him about the last person on the list. I told him I wanted to do this last one without being interrupted. Frankie agreed and prepared his fingers to type furiously.

"Randy Trainer was a jock. In high school and college, he played football in one of the positions that meant hitting and being hit hard. Now, you have to understand, that in our day, helmets weren't much more than an extra layer of padding—not like the high-tech stuff that players have today. Also, Randy was known for doing stupid things like running into walls head first, jumping off the river bank cliffs without knowing how deep the water was, or lifting heavy things, like the principal's VW onto the roof of the administration building with the other jocks as a joke. I mean, the wheel was turning but the hamster had fallen off long ago, if you get my drift. Everyone wondered how he lived as long as he had. That he had an aneurysm didn't surprise me. He must have taken more blows to the head than all the other citizens in town put together.

"I went to the library and read all I could about what caused aneurysms to happen and to burst. I didn't know if the excitement of a major lottery winning as Darcy suggested would be enough to make the thing burst, but I was willing to try. I really couldn't manipulate the numbers so that he'd win, but I could hope he'd get enough numbers from the drawing to make him extremely excited.

"Maggie and I went out and searched the ditches and dumpsters for cans and bottles I could turn in so I'd have enough money to buy the tickets. Ten dollars might not seem like much to most people, but it was a lot to me. And, besides every time I had to buy a ticket, I'd lose a beer. And to me, giving up beer was a major sacrifice. I told Maggie what I was planning over and over. She never sneezed. In fact, she barely looked at me. I should have listened to her.

"Randy was one of the group of guys that I'd partied with all my life. We knew each other but weren't really close. I did know he loved to gamble. I had seen him bet on which of two flies would land on the table first. He would bet on anything. Two days after Darcy left, I saw him having breakfast in the diner and slipped into the booth across from him. He looked up in surprise but didn't tell me to leave. I asked how everything was going. He shook his head and asked, 'What's it to you?' I said that he looked like he needed someone to talk to. Randy sniffed and said, 'Maybe.' He lifted his coffee, took a drink, grimaced and set the cup down again. When he looked at me again, he told me that he was sick and then told me what the doctor told him.

"He said that he needed to stay as calm as he could and not do anything that would cause a blow to the head, like a fall or anything. The doctors told him, the aneurysm was in a place where any sharp blow or any significant rise in blood pressure would cause the thing to burst and he'd die in seconds. He said he was pretty sure they were just trying to scare him. Cops hated when he had any fun and maybe the docs were in on that with them. He took another sip of coffee and grimaced again. 'They've even got me drinking this decaf stuff. Might as well be drinking water from a mud puddle.' I shook my head and clicked my tongue to let him know how bad I felt for him.

"He then started reminiscing about some of the adventures he had been involved in over the course of his long, colorful life. 'Hey, Scabby,' he laughed, 'you remember when we broke into the girls' locker room while they were at PE and stole all their clothes?' I didn't tell him I wasn't a part of that fun, but I laughed like I had been. My laughter encouraged him to go on. He told story after story after mean, long story.

"I waited until he wound down and asked what he'd miss the most. He said he'd miss gambling, betting on the horses or the dogs. Buying a ticket and sitting on the sofa with the tickets in his hand and waiting, full of excitement, to see if his luck was good. He shook his head and said he guessed that was all over. 'Hell, Scabby,' he said, 'they even have me afraid of playing the lottery. And I really feel like I'm due to win. After all the money I put into that, I hate to just give up.'

"I asked how I could help. He just hung his head and stared at the tabletop. He had no idea what he was going to do. 'In fact,' he said, 'I don't even know why I am telling you this.' I

"I gestured to the waitress to refill the coffee and reminded him we'd been friends for a long time. If you couldn't talk to friends, who could you talk to? He scoffed and waited for his cup to be filled.

"We sat quietly drinking our coffee for a few minutes. He'd been quiet for about five minutes when he said, 'You know Scabby. You're right. Let's do this. I have gotten most of my exercise all my life by just pushing my luck.' Then he slammed his fist on the table and yelled 'NO!' At six foot four, 350 pounds, when Randy yelled, everyone in the diner jumped. He stood up and said, 'I'm not going to do this. I'm going to live my life like I always have and, if this thing kills me, so be it. I'm not going to be a wienie about dying.' There were a smattering of applause and people voicing their approval. He dropped a $10 on the table and said, 'Come on Scabby. Let's get plastered.' I slipped out of the booth and he draped his big arm over my shoulders. I felt like a kid under his dad's arm, he was so much bigger than me. We walked out the door together.

"The first thing we did was hit the bar we always used to drink at. Randy acted like a man possessed. He all but ran into the bar, yelling like a banshee. He pulled all the money that he had out of his pocket and told the bartender to set everybody up and keep the booze coming until the money ran out. The bartender looked around. There was no one else there. Randy roared, 'You heard me!'

"We sat and drank and talked for hours. I nursed a few drinks, but Randy tossed back shot after shot followed by beer after beer. By four in the afternoon, Randy was completely wasted. The bartender took the last of the money on the bar and called a cab to take us to his house. With the help of the cabbie, I poured Randy into his bed and then fell onto the couch and slept.

"Darkness had fallen when I woke up. I didn't recognize where I was at first. For a few minutes, I sat on the edge of the saggy old sofa and looked around. When I saw Randy's football trophies from forty years ago still proudly displayed on the sideboard, I remembered what I was supposed to do. I looked at my watch. If I was going to buy lottery tickets, and hopefully winning ones for Randy and me, I needed to go soon. I didn't need to wonder where Randy was. I could hear him snoring down the hall. The sound was impressive. I'm sure the walls didn't really shiver but they seemed to move every time the sound came out of the bedroom.

"I checked my wallet and found that I hadn't spent any of my money that day. I got my jacket and walked down the street to the corner store. There were several people in line to buy tickets when I arrived. Everyone was chattering excitedly about the $6 million dollar pot. I got to the window just in time to buy twenty tickets. When I paid for my chances, lights started flashing on the lotto machine. The clerk said, 'Sorry folks! I'm locked out. I can't sell any more tickets for this drawing.'

"People started grousing and arguing as they milled toward the door. The clerk held his hands up and said there was nothing he could do. The state locked the sales machines when the time for the drawing was close. Behind me a big guy was muttering. As I walked by him, he grabbed my arm and said, 'Hey buddy, I'll pay you twice what you paid for those tickets.' I thought about that idea for just a few nano seconds. He had a hopeful look in his eyes at first, but the look changed as I thought. His brow went from high to low, from hopeful to glowering. I jerked my arm away and ran out the door. Behind me the big guy tried to give chase, but I slipped into the shadows.

"I got back to Randy's house in time for the drawing. I could hear Randy coming down the hall moaning and groaning. I called him and told him to hurry and get out of here. The drawing was about to happen. He stumbled down the hall, telling me to stop yelling. He had a blistering headache. I felt a surge of excitement. Many of the articles I read said that a severe headache was a symptom of aneurysm failure.

"He came in and flopped down. When he saw the lottery program, he said, 'Why are we watching this? We never got to buy tickets.' I smiled at him and said, 'You weren't going to give into this thing, right? So, I decided you shouldn't give up what you said you'd miss most.'

"I pulled the tickets out of my pocket and waved them around. His eyes lit up. I told him, 'You paid for all the entertainment today, so I went and got these tickets for us.' I put half the number of tickets in each hand and said, 'You choose which you want.' He looked at the tickets and said that he always played special numbers. 'Tonight,' I told him, 'you played quick picks.'

"He grabbed the ones in my left hand and turned toward the television. He sat hunkered over the tickets like a wolf guarding his hard-won prey. He picked up the stub of a pencil and licked the lead of the pencil tip nervously as he watched.

"The announcer began to call out the numbers. At the end of the broadcast, I looked at my card. I had one or two numbers, but nothing too exciting. Randy was turned so that his body blocked my view of his ticket. He sat still and said nothing. For a moment, I thought his aneurysm had burst and he had died sitting right there.

"I said, 'Well, no excitement for me. I haven't

got any of those numbers.' Randy slowly turned and faced me. His face was pale and his mouth was moving, like he was trying to say something. He looked like a big-mouthed bass out of water gasping for air. I looked at the ticket in his hand and saw a whole line of circles in the middle of the page. Now equally stunned, I stared back at Randy. Then all hell broke loose.

"Randy jumped to his feet and began screaming, 'I won, I won!' He grabbed me and started dancing around the room. I was too stunned to do anything but let him toss me around. I was torn between letting him get so excited hoping the aneurysm would burst and wanting to take the ticket I paid for away from him. That was my ticket! I'd bought the durned thing and I'd even been willing to fight off a thug to keep it. I needed to get that winning ticket back.

"When he stopped to catch his breath, I asked him, 'We'll split that, right?' Randy stopped dead still. He looked at me and then at the ticket.

'Hell, no!' He said, 'This is mine. I'm set for life!' He started jumping around again. I couldn't believe I was so close to being rich and this giant goombah was between that money and me. I watched him running around the room.

"Without thinking much, I grabbed a broom leaning by the kitchen door and smacked Randy upside the head the next time he stopped to look at the ticket. My arms ached with the impact, but he acted like a fly had lit on his head. He turned around slowly and stared at me. There was murder in his eyes as he stepped forward. I didn't know what to do. I felt rooted in the ground. I knew if he got his hands on me, I'd be dead but I couldn't make my legs move. He got within arm's reach of me and I looked him in the eyes.

"There was something there that scared me and then the thing disappeared. I mean, the angry light was in his eyes and then the light was gone, like someone had shut off something in his brain. My feeble little brain was screaming 'Run!'

to my feet as the towering man fell like dead timber toward me. My feet weren't listening. By the time I realized I was in the fall zone and tried to step aside, I was too late. I felt him hit me and then the room went dark.

"I don't know how long we lay there on the floor, Randy on top of me. I struggled to breathe and felt a pain in my leg that might mean broken bones. I tried to wiggle out from under the fleshy mass but, between his size and my pain, I couldn't. I knew I needed to get help from somewhere.

Randy was old school enough to have a landline phone sitting on the end table. Though it was out of my reach, the broom that I'd used to hit Randy with was on the floor near me. I grabbed the long handle and knocked the phone over. The handset fell towards me. I called 911, told them who and where I was and waited for them to rescue me.

Frankie looked up and said, "Wow. He died?" I nodded.

"As I lay there waiting for the ambulance," I continued, "I realized I should have just let him have the ticket. He'd have been set for life and probably would have moved to some tropical island. I'd have won the big prize and everything would have been fine. Greed is a powerful thing." I looked down at his hand on the floor near my head. The winning ticket was clenched tightly in his fingers. I stretched out my free arm and pried the ticket loose. As I slipped the piece of paper into my shirt pocket, I thought about all the things I could do with the money.

Frankie nodded and turned back to his typing.

"The EMTs showed up soon after I called. I wasn't conscious when they arrived, but I drifted in and out on the way to the hospital. I can only imagine what they thought when they walked in and saw the two of us in a pile on the floor. I thought I heard one say, 'Look at the poor little one. I wonder what he did to make the big guy mad.' Another voice said, 'Maybe they were dancing.'

Then they both laughed. Dancing. Sure."

Frankie laughed. I glared at him. "Sorry," he said and waited for me to talk. "What happened next?"

I gestured around me and said this happened. Frankie looked around him and said, "You mean jail?"

I nodded. "I was in the hospital and then I was here. Everyone said I killed Randy. And then they started saying I'd killed all the others. Remember that snooty nurse back at SnotGun's house, the one who wouldn't let me inside?" Frankie nodded and I said, "Well, she wasn't just snooty, she was nosy too."

CHAPTER

29

Nurse Jenkins:

"The minute I saw Scabby come into the ER, I knew I had to be his nurse. I raced to the gurney and asked the EMT what had happened. He told me that they'd been called to a house to find this little guy and another huge guy in a big pile on the floor. He added the little guy was on the bottom. We transferred the man to the ER bed, and I asked where the other guy was. When the other EMT said he was dead, I must have gotten a look on my face. He continued saying that this guy was on the ground underneath a big guy who was dead. He said the situation looked like the big guy had died of a massive head injury and the little guy had tried to catch him when he fell. I worked hard to keep the disbelief out of my voice and said, 'Really.' The EMT lifted his eyebrows and tilted his head.

"When the two men left to fill the paperwork out at the desk, I pulled the curtains around the bed and began hooking up the monitors. I looked down to see that the patient had his eyes open. I asked if he was in pain. He nodded. I told him he'd have to wait until the doctor saw him before we gave him any more meds but that shouldn't be too long. I asked if he was allergic to anything. He shook his head. I checked the wires and lines again and started tucking the sheet in around him.

"'Well, I said to him, 'you've been a busy one, haven't you?' He looked at me but didn't respond. 'Your name is Scabby, right?' He nodded. I looked him directly in the eye and said, 'Well, Scabby, I know what you did. And I can prove it all.' He closed his eyes and didn't open them again on my shift.

As soon as I got off, I knew I had to get to the sheriff with my evidence. I wasn't going to let this man who'd killed five people get away with murder no matter what the small-town sheriff thought.

Almost Brilliant

CHAPTER

30

"When I strode into the sheriff's office the next morning, he was still behind his desk doing paperwork. I wondered just how much paperwork such a small town could generate. When he looked up, he sat back in his chair and gave me a half smile.

"'Nurse Jenkins, what can I do for you?'

"I refused to smile back. Instead, I dropped my bag of evidence on his desk and said, 'It's more like what I can do for you, Sheriff!'

"He picked up the bag and separated the

items with his meaty fingers. The nurse's hat, the bag of chocolate goo, copies of news reports on the preacher, the strip of monitor paper, reports from the night Mr. Trainer and Miss Savannah had been in the ER, and my notes connecting those times with the times Scabby had been in the hospital. 'What is all this?'

"I pulled up a chair and said, 'Sheriff, you have a murderer loose in your town and that is the proof.'

"He dropped the bag and sat back in his chair. For a long moment he stared at me, using no doubt the same stare he'd used on the few criminals he has ever interrogated. Well, he'd met his match in me. I returned his stare with my own stony glare, honed by all my years of dealing with patients who thought they knew better than me.

"He broke first and asked, 'And who might the murderer be?'

"'A man known locally as Scabby." The jerk

nearly fell off his chair he was so taken aback. Then he began to laugh like a braying mule. I sat back and crossed my arms over my chest. I was used to waiting out men who thought they knew more than me. When he finished laughing, he had tears rolling down his cheeks. He used his sleeves to dab at his eyes.

"'I gotta hand it to you, Ms. Jenkins. You really know how to lighten up a conversation.'

"'I am serious, Sheriff.'

"When he'd composed himself, he pushed his chair back and stood up. Without another word, he walked across the room and began to make fresh coffee. Over his shoulder, he said, 'I'm assuming you drink coffee.'

"'Black, no sugar, no cream.' I heard him sniff. He stood with his back to me and watched the deep brown liquid fill the carafe. When the pot was full, he picked up two mugs, a fistful of sugar packets and the pot before returning to his side of the desk. I sat and watched him dump 6 packets of sugar into a mug before filling both of them with coffee. He lifted his cup to his lips, sipped noisily and put the cup down. When he finally seemed to have collected his thoughts, he looked at me again.

"'So, fill me in. What do you think is going on?'

"'I haven't figured out exactly why the hat is there yet. But if you look at the underside, there are hairs stuck in the band. They are blonde. Obviously not mine,' as I indicated my sensible short dark brown style.

"The sheriff looked at me. 'And you think Scabby snuck into the sick room wearing a nurse's hat?'

"I haven't figured out exactly why the hat is there yet. But if you look at the underside, there are hairs stuck in the band. They are blonde. Obviously not mine."

"'Ok, what's next?' He pulled the bag of melted 'chocolate' out of the large bag and looked at me with raised eyebrows.

"'Do you remember when Faith Chandler slipped in her apartment, hit her head and died?'

"The sheriff nodded. 'Simple slip and fall. Happens to old people all the time.'

"I couldn't figure out why Miss Faith, who was diabetic and had a morbid fear of gaining the weight she lost back, would have had a chocolate cake in her apartment. But when I was cleaning up, I got a little of the chocolate on my hand. Without thinking, I licked the icing off my finger. The taste was odd. I couldn't place it until a week or so later.' I looked at the sheriff but he seemed to have no questions so I continued, 'I went back and looked at the security tapes for the building later in the day and saw a man and a woman carrying a box across the lobby while I was away from the desk. That was about an hour before someone called 911 from her apartment.'

"He tilted his head to the right as if to tell me to go on. I took the bag from him and spread the papers out on his desk. 'This is the strip from the heart monitor that was in Mr. Remington's room. See how the lines are regular until right here.' I put my finger on a spot near the end of the tape. 'Suddenly they begin to jump erratically until the machine was shut off. Something frightened him badly to make that happen.' I told him that Scabby had come to see him a day or so earlier and was not happy at all that I wouldn't let him in. I could tell he didn't see the connection yet.

"The sheriff nodded and picked up the next piece of paper. He looked at me askance.

"'That is a news report about a preacher who was killed by a truck.'

"'That was Beefy McGuire. Obviously, an accident.'

"'Not according to the gossips at the diner.' The sheriff barely stopped himself from scoffing but he said nothing. 'They said he was a teetotaler but that he reeked of alcohol at the scene of the accident.'

"The sheriff confirmed that fact. 'He'd been

drinking and no one knows exactly why. But he used to be a drinker in his youth.'

"'I know,' I said. 'The ladies of the church were very upset that he was hanging around with his old pal Scabby again. Scabby being a known drunk and all.' I think that finally got his attention. He drew a legal pad out of his drawer and picked up the pen he'd abandoned when I came in. He made a few notes and nodded for me to continue.

"I showed him the notes from my conversation with Miss Savannah. 'She said she thought she heard another person in the room besides the missing census taker. After I talked to her, I went down to check something on her chart. On a whim, I did a search for this Scabby person. I found out he was admitted to the ER the same night as Miss Faith's accident with severe dehydration. The notes said there was a woman with him who said he'd accidently eaten a chunk of Ex-lax she'd left on her counter. A bolt of lightning hit me and

I remembered the chocolate goop in the baggie. That was the odd taste I couldn't place.' I sat back and waited for him to quit writing. He leaned back and tapped his pen on the pad for a few minutes. I let him mull on that a bit and then continued.

"The last bit fell into place last night when Scabby was brought into the ER with a man named Randy Trainer. Apparently, the two of them were watching a lottery drawing and one of them hit the big win. I'm not sure what happened between them, but Randy's dead from a burst aneurysm in his head ... which according to the gossips, everyone knew about because he announced the fact the day before when he was in the diner having breakfast with, in their words, that 'ne'er-do-well Scabby'.' I waggled my eyebrows suggestively.

"The sheriff took a deep breath and blew it out. 'This is quite a nice pile of circumstantial evidence, Miss Jenkins, but I don't think this is enough to arrest poor old Scabby and get him sent to prison for murder.'

"'I might think so too, sheriff. If I hadn't seen this.' I pulled another newspaper clipping out of my pocket and slid the wrinkled page across the desk. 'Look at the names on this list.'

"I watched the significance of the list dawn on the sheriff's face as he finally made the connection. 'I'm not saying we have enough evidence here, Miss Jenkins. But I think we need to bring Scabby in to for a talk.'

"I leaned back in my chair and gave him my most beatific smile. I loved the feeling when I proved a man wrong, especially a vainglorious man like this one. I watched as he stood up again and walked over to the radio console. He called his deputy and told him to go over to the hospital. Scabby was to be arrested and brought to the station for questioning as soon as the doctors released him. I heard the deputy scoff and argue, but the sheriff finally said, 'Just arrest him.' He disconnected the call and returned to the desk.

He stood there and looked at the pile of evidence. Then he looked at me and offered his hand. I stood to shake it. 'I don't know what will happen, Ms. Jenkins, but I'll let the DA know about all this. He will probably want to talk with you.'

"'I will be here ... ooo, and the name is Nurse Jenkins.' I smiled and turned my back on him. I heard him snort as I closed the door behind me."

CHAPTER

Frankie came into the cell on the morning before I was going to be put on trial. I waited while he set up. He gave Maggie a pat and then looked at me sadly. He asked, "So we are done?"

"Well," I said, "Except for a few little details, like how the trial turns out and what the city council decides. I just need to make sure you understand everything."

He nodded. I asked if he had any questions. He said no. He'd typed everything up last night and he was ready to take the story to the editor as soon as I told him he could.

He asked, "Did everything happen the way you planned? Do you think they will give you the prize? The celebration is tomorrow and you are indeed the oldest person still in town after all."

I had to think about that idea. I said, "Pete told me that the council was meeting this morning to discuss the situation."

He said he'd love to be a little mouse in the corner to listen to them all pointing fingers and talking about what to do with the prize.

"Pete had told me," I continued, "that they were calling the prize blood money and wanted to do something else instead of giving the money to me."

When he arrested me, Pete had shaken his head and said he had to hand it to me. He'd never seen those staid, proper people in such a dither. He said I shook them up good. If I'd really done all this just so I would be remembered, then I'd absolutely accomplished my goal.

"The truth of it all," I told the kid, as I thought about all that had happened was, "if I had left everything alone, I would have won anyway. When you look back on the whole thing, they all died or left on their own. I was just near-by."

"I mean, look at SnotGun. The poor old guy's heart was so bad off that he'd have died soon enough. The way I see the situation, if anything, I gave him a last few minutes of joy. Not the way I'd planned but just the same, he died laughing instead of laying up there all alone with no one to share his last days with. I did him a favor by being there."

"Faith was another success story. I may have had more to do with her passing, but still I feel like I did her a service. She was alone and living in a prison of her own making. She'd deprived herself of the one thing she loved the most – her baking. I was there to celebrate her last birthday and brought her a joyous gift to share. That she fell was an act of God and that had nothing to do with me. Who's to say she wouldn't have fallen that day even if I hadn't been there. I mean, like they say when your number is up, your number is up."

"And Beefy? Well, my old friend was miserable. He was living a life of being hen-pecked and pushed around by a woman who had no idea who he was. I wish I'd been with him that last night. I would have loved to have had one last drink with him. But when you get right down to the facts, I had nothing to do with his death."

I stopped and looked at Frankie. I couldn't tell if he was buying my version of the facts. "Really," I said, "all I did was make him see what the rest of his life would be like." Frankie shook his head, but I ignored him and moved on.

"Then there was Miss Savannah. She was alone in that house. Blind and scared to go outside. People were taking advantage of her and she was too good a person to have that happening to her. I just helped her decide to leave that dusty old house and move to be with people who loved her. She will probably be happier for the rest of her life than she ever had been before." Frankie shrugged his shoulder reluctantly.

"Admit it," I demanded. "Even you have to agree that she's better off." To his credit, Frankie said that he had to give me that one.

"As for Randy, think about the joy he had for those last few moments of his life. He was dancing around like a ten-year-old kid in a candy shop. He was probably happier than he'd ever been in his life when the aneurysm burst. He never knew what happened."

Frankie thought over the last bit and said, "There is one thing that's not finished." I shook my head not being able to think of anything I hadn't told him. He looked at me and said "What about Darcy?"

That took me aback. I thought for a minute or two. "She's still in the city," I told him. "I haven't talked to her since I was put in here. I called her the night I got arrested and told her what had happened. She wanted to come back, but I told her to stay with her friend. She cried and said he was so sick, and really needed her but she wanted to be there for me too. I told her that I was going to try to keep her out of the limelight and, if she stayed there, maybe no one would look at her."

I asked Frankie for a piece of paper and his pencil. I scribbled down a number and handed the scrap back to him. "If I get sentenced to prison, I want you to call her and tell her to stay away. I'm trusting you to keep her away from here." I stood up and asked, "Can I trust you?" I reached under my pillow and pulled out an envelope addressed to Darcy. "I need you to mail this and forget you ever saw the address."

Frankie walked over to me and took the paper and the envelope. He looked at the scribbling for a few long moments and then he nodded. I saw his Adam's apple bounce as he swallowed hard.

"So that's everything, Kid. Unless you have any questions, you can see how I wasn't to blame for any of this. Take the story home and finish the last bit up. Tell your editor that you want to be at the trial and write the last part based on what happens there. After everything is over, we'll get together again. I really want to read the finished product. I think this story has the makings of a Pulitzer Prize winner."

Frankie laughed and turned to gather his things for probably the last time. When he was done, he came back to where I was sitting and stuck his hand out to shake mine. I struggled up. When I took the big meat hook, he pulled me into a hug and whispered, "Thank you." When he leaned back, he didn't release my hand. "Thank you for trusting me with all this."

I nodded and looked down at my hand. "I'm going to need that," I laughed. He gave a rueful smile, dropped my hand and leaned down to grab his laptop case. He walked out the door without looking back. He was halfway down the hall when I called him back. I limped across the cell and got Maggie's leash. She jumped up on the bed and waited for me to put it on her. I clipped the leash and scooped her up for a good hugging. Her pink tongue licked my face as I smelled her doggy fur one last time.

When Frankie got to the door, I put Maggie down and said, "Take her with you. She's gonna be lonesome here with me in court all day." Frankie took the leash and turned to leave.

I watched them go down the hall and listened as he talked to the sheriff. When I heard the door close in the distance, I went back to my bunk and stretched out with my hands behind my head. I propped my aching leg up on the end of the bed and I patted the side of the cot. I pretended I could feel Maggie jump up beside me and snuggle into the crook of my arm like she always did. I smiled and closed my eyes.

EPILOGUE

Frankie:

I found the old man in his cell the next morning. He'd died in his sleep. He lay there, smiling off in to the air as if he hadn't a care in the world and I guess he didn't.

I called the sheriff down. He stood in the cell door, took his hat off and said, "Well, I'll be damned. I guess he got what he wanted."

"How's that?" I asked.

"Well, he's never going to have to worry about food or a place to sleep ever again. And that's all anyone wants, right?"

After they had removed the body, I stayed in the cell a few minutes longer. I was going to miss Scabby a lot. I walked over to the shelf where he kept his book and wondered what was going to become of them. I moved a well-worn copy of *Great Expectations*. A sheet of paper folded four times fell off the shelf. It was addressed to "The Kid." I opened the first fold to see:

"Hey, Frankie,

If you're reading this, I guess I died. I knew you'd ask if you could have the books! Thanks for making my last days less lonely, but I have bad news for you. Everything I told you was a big whopping lie. But it was a hell of a story, right? You're a good writer and you need to go to college. Send this book to some big publisher and make us both famous.

I guess I won the big prize after all, didn't I"? And all I had to do was wait.

Best of luck, Scabby"

Inside the second fold of the paper, I found a winning lottery ticket.

Printed in the USA
CPSIA information can be obtained
at www.ICGtesting.com
CBHW031655040424
6298CB00006B/22